Other books by Jeff Deitering

*Meet Hook*
*Hooked Up*


*Hooligan from the Hills: Growing Up Ornery in*
*Iowa's Loess Hills*
*(Nonfiction as Jeffrey D. Deitering)*

# On the Hook

By Jeff Deitering

First Edition

Jeff Deitering
P.O. Box 315
Lawrence, KS  66044

www.jeffdeitering.com

To Sandy and our kitties.

# ACKNOWLEDGMENTS

A big thank you to Jes, Anzia, and Dana, who hooked me up to the notion of writing these stories. My sincerest appreciation to my beta readers Cindy, Joey, Nina, and Tony. Thank you to real-life safe cracker, Ken Dunckel, for responding to my unusual request for technical assistance. A shout out to Rick and the staff of Johnny's Tavern North for putting up with me writing the last half of this book at their bar. Once again, thanks to Eric for creating a great cover from my crude sketch. A huge thanks to my editor, Ami, for proving over and over how imperfect I am. Thank you so much to Barbra Annino for allowing her characters, Stacy Justice and Thor, to make cameos. Most of all, thank you to all the Kansas City Metro pet rescue organizations and their volunteers who take care of far too many of Patch's friends. Adopt and adopt often.

# ACKNOWLEDGMENTS

A big thank you to Jes, Anzia, and Dana, who hooked me up to the notion of writing these stories. My sincerest appreciation to my beta readers Cindy, Joey, Nina, and Tony. Thank you to real-life safe cracker, Ken Dunckel, for responding to my unusual request for technical assistance. A shout out to Rick and the staff of Johnny's Tavern North for putting up with me writing the last half of this book at their bar. Once again, thanks to Eric for creating a great cover from my crude sketch. A huge thanks to my editor, Ami, for proving over and over how imperfect I am. Thank you so much to Barbra Annino for allowing her characters, Stacy Justice and Thor, to make cameos. Most of all, thank you to all the Kansas City Metro pet rescue organizations and their volunteers who take care of far too many of Patch's friends. Adopt and adopt often.

# Chapter One

The shapely woman in a very tiny bikini crooked a finger and beckoned. Her flowing hair, killer legs, and tan as brown as a UPS truck looked vaguely familiar but I couldn't quite place her face; probably a movie or television star or...or, ya know, it really didn't matter because she was totally hot and motioning to me. Probably me. I glanced from side to side to make sure she wasn't looking at someone else, nodding smugly to myself when I found no one else around.

My eyes returned to her; I noticed for the first time the gorgeous woman held a bottle of caramel sauce and a Nerf football. I don't know how I missed that initially but I was suddenly all kinds of excited. She raised a hand and slowly puckered her lips. She blew a kiss my direction. My knees quaked and threatened to give out.

I walked awkwardly toward her, my feet sinking into the ground as though I walked through a pool of warm peanut butter. I struggled through the muck, stopping in front of the erotic goddess. She raised her hand to her lips again. I frowned. Her hand was covered in floofy gray fur, like she wore a glove for a wookie costume. My brow furrowed as I looked up and to the right, pondering just how messy the fur and caramel sauce would get. I quickly decided I didn't care and returned my gaze back to her. She smiled mischievously then drew back her furry hand and smacked me right on the nose. I lurched awake to find the real assailant sitting on my chest.

"Patch, seriously, why?" I mumbled to the gray, one-eyed cat with extraordinary intuition. He ignored my question, instead reaching out with a paw and smacking my nose again. He quickly scampered away.

I squinted. My eyes gradually adjusted to the faint morning light. The glow of a late December sunrise overwhelmed the streetlights outside my window, slowly changing the hue of my bare bedroom walls from cold blue to a warm peach.

Patch jumped onto my cluttered nightstand and stared at me. His twitching tail brushed against the clock radio. The glowing digits repeatedly blinked 12:00, a stroboscopic reminder I needed to relearn how to set it.

Patch batted at the truck keys I'd left next to the uninformative clock. I knew what ornery thought ran through his head.

"Patch," I said, "knock it off."

He stopped briefly and tilted his head. His whiskers twitched suggesting I'd chosen my words poorly. He swatted the keys one last time. They skittered off the table and clattered onto the floor.

I sighed. Knocking things onto the floor was a specialty he usually reserved for glasses of water or open bottles of beer.

Having defeated another inanimate foe, he posed proudly on the nightstand and winked slowly at me with his one eye. Or, maybe

2

he just blinked – I'm never completely sure. The furry smirk on his face strongly suggested wink though. He looked down and began licking a front paw.

I rolled across the bed and reached for the keys that had landed a foot away from the nightstand, almost beyond my reach. My fingertips grazed the keyring but I was too lazy to crawl out of bed. I stretched just a little further…and paid for it with my lower back spasming.

"Aaaargh!"

I gritted my teeth and snagged the keys. I dropped them onto the nightstand then flopped back onto the pillows. Patch never stopped his grooming while I contorted in pain.

I shot him a glare. He paused for a moment then pawed at the television remote.

"Really?" I asked while reaching for the remote. Another spasm shot through my back as I clenched it.

"Ungh."

I recoiled in pain like I'd grabbed a live electric wire. "Mother son of a rat fudrucking bastard..."

Patch interrupted my incoherent swearing with a single meow.

I looked at him in confusion. He meowed again. I bit my lip to ignore another spasm of pain to puzzle out what my cat's meow meant.

Patch is a special cat. A very special cat. I was never a cat person but my ex–girlfriend no, I mean my very ex-girlfriend, convinced me I needed one back when she wasn't yet an ex.

I met Patch at the Kansas City Pet Project animal shelter. They told me he had a tough few months as a kitten on the streets of Kansas City; he was pretty banged up and missing an eye when one of the shelter's volunteers found him. They'd taken extremely good care of him and nursed him back to health – minus the one eye of course.

I soon learned that for a one-eyed kitty he seems to see things better than most people. He first got my attention at the shelter by clawing his way up my jeans and scratching at my cell phone until it rang, predicting the incoming call several seconds in advance. Impressed by his parlor trick, I adopted him on the spot.

Patch has performed that cell phone trick way too many times to be just coincidence. However, because he rarely "talks" and I'd never seen him paw at any gadget besides my cellphone, he had my attention. I begrudgingly hit the power button on the clicker.

I expected to see an infomercial for a miracle wang enhancer. Don't judge me – I've heard those ads for clinically tested and guaranteed-to-work pills often run in the early morning hours. However, instead of willy stiffeners, I found a replay of the 10 o'clock news.

I rarely watch the news. Mostly because it's usually filled with really bad stuff and so little of it is actually newsworthy. I yawned and aimed the remote at the set to turn it off. Patch yowled. I looked at him and saw his stare remained fixed on the television. I looked back and discovered he was watching my boss, Jimmy Penders, on the screen. Penders talked to the reporter in front of a dilapidated old building. Surrounding Jimmy and the reporter was a small group of business-casual dressed people, all protected by new, sparkling white hardhats.

4

I moved closer to the TV to see where exactly my enigmatic employer was.

Patch let out another meow.

From the corner of my eye, I saw Patch shift his interest to one of my cellphones. I sighed in advance of the inevitable.

Seconds later the Jimmy Phone – a relatively low-featured smartphone that only receives work calls – jangled to life.

I glanced at the screen; it simply read, "BLOCKED". It always does. But, it's almost always Jimmy's larger than life business manager, Stanley, calling on Jimmy's behalf, so I had a pretty fair idea who was on the other end.

If it was my personal cell phone I would have ignored the call and went back to sleep. I learned long ago, though, it's impossible to ignore Jimmy Penders. Or Stanley. Besides, I practically saved Stanley's life once; since then he and I were pretty tight.

I hit <ANSWER>.

"Hey, ya, Stan. What's up with you this fine morning?" I asked with a lot more cheeriness than I felt. A flutter in my lumbar disagreed with my assessment of the morning.

An annoyed Stanley replied, "Are you ever going to remember to enter the code?"

The morning fog in my noggin was slow to clear. Code sounded familiar but I didn't grasp his meaning.

"Whadda ya mean code, Stan?"

"The ignition code, you idiot. You tried starting my truck without the code again."

The mist drifting through my gray matter thinned – but only slightly. For a couple of months while Stanley recovered from the car accident from which I'd saved him, I'd been driving's his Escalade. The paranoid bastard had a keypad installed in it. I was supposed to enter 1-9-8-5 into the pad after getting inside the truck or an alert text would be sent to his phone. He was right: I didn't always remember to do that. I forgot it a lot, actually. However, that didn't explain this wake-up call.

"Um, Stan? What the hell are you talking about?"

The phone's tiny speaker popped and crackled with his screaming reply.

"Hook! What the hell are you doing in my truck?!"

Patch pawed at the truck keys on the nightstand then looked away.

Aw, shit.

Chapter Two

What the hell indeed. When Stanley totaled a car a few months ago, I practically saved his life. We'd been almost inseparable buds ever since.

But by "totaled a car" I don't mean he crashed one. I mean a sociopathic hitman tried to run him down – run him down with a SMART car – no less. The glorified Hotwheel merely bounced off Stanley's former-fullback physique and burst into flames. And, by "saved his life" I mean after Stanley pulled himself away from the smoking vehicle, I held open the door of the taxi that rushed him to the hospital.

Still, we'd been on somewhat friendly terms since then. He'd even entrusted me with some of his administrative duties many of which included running errands in his Escalade. His angry wake-up call, though, was almost like we had regressed to...to...

"HOOK! WHERE THE HELL ARE YOU TAKING MY TRUCK?!"

...to like we were before the accident.

Dammit.

"Stan, I tell ya, I'm really not in the truck," I said rolling off the bed, "I'm, uh, still in my bedroom."

I walked across the room. I looked from my 5th floor loft in Kansas City's historic Western Auto building into the secure parking lot below.

"Aaand your truck is still down in my–"

The sight of Stan's Escalade zipping out of my parking lot cut me short. A black coat sleeve emerged from the passenger window and waggled a middle finger good-bye to me. In an instant, only tire tracks remained in the dusting of snow on the ground.

"Son of a bitch. Stan, somebody just drove off with your truck."

A tortured sigh resembling the snort of a charging rhinoceros blasted through the phone.

"Why else would I call? Of course it's gone. We logged the keypad error five minutes ago."

I looked at Patch. He still sat beside the truck keys, cleaning a paw. I smiled. The joke was on the thieves. Even bypassing the ignition keypad wouldn't disable the lojack–

"DAMMIT!" Stanley shouted, "Now the tracking signal is gone!"

He snorted again. Patch rested a paw on the missing truck's keys and gave me an I-tried-to-warn-you look. I glared back at him.

"Ok, Stan. I'll call the police and report it right away."

"DON'T! Don't bother. Get dressed. Be in front of your building in ten minutes."

"Sure, ten min–"

CLICK.

Patch had turned his attention back to the TV remote. I finished the call as though Stanley hadn't hung up on me. "–utes. Yes, ten minutes. I'll be ready. Talk with ya later, Stan." I made a big production of hitting <END> and looked at Patch. He tilted his head with fuzzy disdain. He didn't buy it for even a second. No one ever does.

I shook off Stanley's gruffness. At least he didn't threaten to rip out my spleen like he used to do at the end of every call. I dropped the phone onto the bed and changed into the least fragrant jeans and flannel shirt I could find in the pile of dirty clothes composting on my floor.

I swiped the remote from Patch's playing paws and aimed it at the television. Another angle of Jimmy and the rest of the group in hardhats flashed onto the set. I managed to read "Developers Find History Mystery" in the crawl at the bottom of the screen.

Patch meowed.

I looked at him and agreed, "Yes, that is a pretty cheesy rhyme."

I returned my attention to the television but my boss was replaced with a story about a snow skiing badger. I fired the remote's <OFF> button and killed the puff piece.

I stuffed the phones and truckless keys into my pockets then walked into the small living-dining-kitchen area of my loft. Patch jumped onto the counter next to the sink and supervised me as I freshened his food and water dishes and scooped his litter box. I tossed

9

him a couple of nuggets of Kitty Krak treats. He wolfed them down as I pulled on my old Redwing boots and faded Carhartt coat. He was recleaning his front paws when I slipped out the door.

I checked my watch in the hallway. I had two minutes to get outside. Stanley is always irrationally obsessed with deadlines and his tone of voice strongly hinted he might actually tear out one of my vital organs if I was late. Maybe two.

I punched the call button for the elevator but was second-guessing myself for not taking the stairs when it didn't appear immediately. Even without Patch to warn me, I knew the Jimmy Phone would ring in two minutes and one second if I wasn't standing at the front door of my building.

The elevator finally arrived. My rotund munchkin 3rd floor neighbor, Mrs. Crabetts, was in it holding her dog, a yappy Maltese-Shih Tzu-Chihuahua mix of a mutt. The dog wore a heavy knit sweater that made it look like Mr. Rogers reincarnated as a mop. I rolled my eyes as the doors slid shut.

"Alone this morning?" she asked with a sharp tone of disapproval.

I'd recently started dating Dea, a very pretty neighbor who also lives on the 3rd floor. Patch adores her and, in his own feline way, even played matchmaker for us.

I was in a bit of trouble with my psychotic ex-girlfriend – the typical held-at-gunpoint kind of trouble. Patch – who isn't allowed to go outside of our loft – managed to slip past Psycho Ex and get Dea. He scratched on Dea's door to get her attention then led her back to my apartment where she tazed the ever-living shit out of my ex. We've been dating ever since. Dea and I, I mean. Neither of us ever figured out how Patch got from the 5th floor to the 3rd floor though.

Before we even had our second date, our relationship caught the attention of the ever-vigilant building busybody, Mrs. Crabetts, and her best friend, the equally snoopy Mrs. Sweeney. Both are very protective of Dea and greatly disapprove of me – something they make very clear whenever they "accidentally" bump into one of us after a sleepover. I think the old biddies stake out our lofts just so they can cluck their tongues and feign horror at the thought of me morally corrupting "their" little girl.

Dea was already at work at the coffee shop she owned; Mrs. Crabetts damn well knew that, but was jerking my chain. I jerked back.

"Yes, Mrs. Crabetts, it's just me. Patch decided to stay in today."

She scrunched up her face like she'd bitten into a rancid éclair. I ruined her morning by not mentioning Dea. Her mutt whimpered at Patch's name. Even though Patch is supposed to stay in the loft, he has escaped a few other times. Usually his adventures are short-lived forays into the hallway. However, one time he cornered Mrs. Crabetts' dog and swatted him on the snout.

The elevator stopped at the 2nd floor. Mrs. Crabetts exited with her pain-in-the-ass pooch.

"Say hello to Mrs. Sweeney for me," I said with a broad smile as she tottered away. She didn't even turn to acknowledge me.

I could feel the phone ringing in my pocket. Instead of answering it, I jabbed at the <DOOR CLOSE> button repeatedly trying to urge the doors shut. I checked my watch as the elevator car rattled down the remaining story to ground level. I was two minutes late when the doors parted.

I power-walked to the lobby door. The phone rang again. I pulled it from my pocket and answered while stepping outside.

"You're late," Stanley's voice said dully. "Get in the car and try not to lose it."

He hung up before I could ask "what car?"

I stepped outside into a meat locker of a morning. The dry air was dead still. The mucus in my nostrils flash-froze making my boogers feel like frigid sand. A thin film of frost and powdery snow reflected the lightening sky giving my neighborhood an Ansel Adams appearance. Leafless trees stood motionless against the dark sky like anorexic supermodels voguing for the paparazzi. The brick office buildings surrounding my loft were dark and lifeless; their inhabitants gone for the holidays. I smiled: Kansas City can be very peaceful on early winter mornings, you know, when most of the people stay inside.

A blaring locomotive whistle shattered the serenity.

The ear-piercing blast wasn't from a passing freight train, though. It was my signal to get a move on.

I sighed and trudged toward my ride.

Chapter Three

The source of the obnoxious racket was an 80s era, crimson red, Chevy Impala with "Drop Off Taxi Co." stenciled in yellow on the door. Even if it wasn't the only running car on the street, I knew it was there for me.

The cab is owned and driven by Nikola Andropov, an enigmatic, 60ish, pudgy fan of plaid pants and polyester polos. Some people say he's a Communist diplomat who defected from East Germany the day before the Berlin Wall fell. Others say he is a former KGB assassin. I even overheard some guy at a bar say Nik was an NSA mole in the CIA who infiltrated the GRU – that guy was pretty drunk though.

Nik describes himself as a "common immigrant" with a weakness for good barbecue. I once saw him quick-draw a silenced Makarov pistol from his waistband and nearly whack a rabbit hopping through a meadow. If that's how a common immigrant reacts when startled by Bugs Bunny then who am I to question his past?

Nik bought his car – a used police interceptor – at a city auction shortly after arriving in the United States. The former police cruiser was already crazy fast but he made some additional engine improvements creating the speediest car-for-hire in Kansas City. He quickly painted over the midnight blue with colors he found more comfortable. I know for a fact he washes and waxes it every Saturday morning – even when it rains. The locomotive horn was a recent addition to his baby; he was quite proud of that particular modification.

Despite creating arguably the sweetest cab in the metro, the "For Hire" sign on its roof is perpetually unlit. Although Nik is an independent cabbie, he generally only drives Jimmy Penders' friends and clients.

I shuffled up to the taxi. Since we're friends, I dropped into the front seat rather than the rear. Nik was dressed for winter. Oh, he was still wearing his usual Chelsea boots and polyester dress pants, but he conceded to the weather and also wore a wool newsboy cap and a puffy insulated coat. I didn't even know that Members Only made winter coats.

"Morning, Nik," I said.

He grunted in reply without looking at me. He flipped the shifter into Drive and launched us down the street before I finished buckling my seatbelt.

"Friends" might be too strong of a word. We're probably more colleagues than friends, really.

Being the dead week between Christmas and New Year's Eve – and god-awful early in the morning – the streets were as empty as a politician's soul. The public works trucks had coated the streets with a minimal smattering of sand and salt. Nik zipped over the grit as though at were dry pavement. The back tires broke free for a moment when we turned onto 13th Street. Nik took his right hand from the wheel and rested his arm across the top of the front seat. He looked at me. I gripped the door handle in preparation for the inevitable accident.

"Zo, you looze Ztanley'z truck, da?"

I often wondered why after nearly forty years in the Midwest his accent is still heavily East Bloc. I think he sometimes thickens it on purpose. It's something I think but never dare ask.

We slipped around the intersection of 18th Street and Grand Avenue. Nik never even checked the traffic signal – it was well into the yellow cycle. As the ass-end of his car began to slide, he goosed the gas and deftly straightened us out. My grip on the door handle tightened.

"Um, I didn't really lose it. Someone took it. I think maybe Stick or one of his guys grabbed it to work on."

Nik exploded with a laugh that sounded like Santa Claus when he kicks a lazy elf in the ass.

"Nyet. Zteek iz vaiting for you vith Jeemy and Ztan."

Super. Jimmy called a meeting of his inner circle – the three people he trusts. And me.

Stick is another one of Jimmy's employees. He's a thug from Canada who runs a secret garage in the West Bottoms. The West Bottoms is an old industrial neighborhood next to the Missouri River in a flood prone part of the city. Stick and his gang of gargantuan grease monkeys maintain, repair, and upgrade vehicles for most of the metro's rich and famous. I'm pretty sure Stick's henchmen did the engine modifications on Nik's car – and probably installed the locomotive horn, too.

Nik deftly skated us to the Interstate Building at 13th and Locust Streets. Buffalo Bill's Bar and Grill – my favorite watering hole and Jimmy's favorite meeting space – occupies half the ground floor of the historic, five-story, brick office building. As we neared the building, he jammed on his brakes and slid the cab into Bill's parking lot at the south side of the bar. Nik skidded the cab through 3/4 of a doughnut in the mostly empty lot coming to a stop in an open parking space perpendicular to the old brick building.

Common immigrant my ass.

Nik was out of the car and striding across the lot before I got my door open. I stepped onto the half inch of fluff that blanketed the lot. Next to us was black Subaru Impreza with an obnoxiously large air scoop on its hood and windows tinted as dark as a welding visor. That was the crazy Canuck Stick's ride.

A sign affixed to the building declared our parking spot was "reserved all hours – all days."

"Hey, Nik, I think you're in somebody's spot," I called out to him.

Nik raised a fistful of keys and waved off my concern. As he disappeared around the corner of the building, a very retro security system whoop-whooped from under the hood of the car. I don't think he cared whose spot he took.

I turned away from the sign that apparently didn't apply to Nik and followed. My first step was onto a patch of ice. My left foot glided across the ice and arced upward like Charlie Brown missing another Thanksgiving kick. My right knee exploded in pain before buckling. The thin film of icy powder didn't appreciably soften the underlying pavement; I thudded ass-to-asphalt onto the parking lot. A small cloud of snow billowed away from my keister like I'd farted in a pillow factory.

I whipped my head side to side looking for witnesses. Fortunately, it was still well before opening time and no one saw my slip-up; my pride wasn't bruised as much as my backside.

I propped myself onto my feet and walked gingerly across the rest of the lot to the sidewalk at the corner of the building. Bill's has a corner entrance – the other corner fifty knee-aching feet away. By the time I limped my way to the door Nik was already inside. I paused for a deep breath and trudged through the doorway.

I like Bill's a lot. I know I can go there for a beer or three and, except for the occasional grunt of acknowledgement from a regular, people leave each other, and more importantly, me, the hell alone. It's close enough to my loft that I can walk home when the need arises but far enough away that I don't drink myself stupid. Not very often, anyway. It's also far enough away from the new Power and Light entertainment district that the hipster-slacker crowd stays away. With the city and county courthouses, a police station, and several government buildings within a block the daytime crowd is mostly minor government functionaries, cops, robbers, or, worse yet, attorneys – all of whom prefer seclusion and not being seen.

Bill's thrives on the "not being seen" part: stepping into the bar is like walking into a root cellar that's inside the basement of a cave. Even though one wall is entirely windows looking onto 13th Street and another wall is filled with windows looking onto Locust Street, the glass is heavily tinted to keep most of that pesky daylight out.

When 100-watt incandescent bulbs were still plentiful, enough of them were in the ceiling fixtures you could all too easily see details in the decor such as the dark wood paneling that was once very ornate but now just stained and patron-beaten. The black walnut tables, chairs, and barstools looked as though they were once part of a fancier joint but kept only to help suck unflattering photons from the room. Maroon floor tiles absorb the remaining available light, holding it hostage until their ransom of a coat of wax is paid. A lone stuffed buffalo head attached to the sidewall paneling stands as a silent reminder of the place's name, its curly mat of brown fur graying with decades of dust.

Over the years as the hundred-watters burned out, the few that were replaced were changed out with increasingly dimmer and dimmer bulbs from the Dollar Store closeout bin, slowly making the bar the envy of all the city's movie theaters. I doubt the patrons noticed the gradual change; if they did it was with a silent and increasingly difficult-to-detect note of appreciation.

I leaned against the end of the bar to let my eyes adjust to the darkness and my nose adjust to the odor. Although the city of Kansas City banned smoking indoors in 2008, the previous seven decades of

18

cigars and unfiltered cigarettes left their mark: Bill's still carries the aroma of a tobacco fueled bonfire.

The lone flat panel television at the opposite end of the bar flickered with the morning edition of ESPN's *Sports Center*. Rex, the surly old bastard of a bartender, washed chipped beer mugs in the glow of the Plays of the Day.

"How's it going, Rex?"

He paused. Turning slowly, he gave me the icy glower of a man interrupted in the middle of a very rigid routine. He returned his focus back to the dirty glassware and resumed rinsing. He didn't tell me to go fuck myself so I knew he was actually having a pretty good morning. I didn't push it by ordering a beer, though.

Jimmy and his paranoid inner circle faced me from their usual table at the far corner of the room. Jimmy, dressed in business casual navy slacks and a white cotton Oxford, sat with his back to the wall next to the seldom-used rear exit.

His rhinoceros-sized business manager, Stanley, in an extra-extra-extra-large maroon Nike warm-up suit and black ball cap, was on Jimmy's left. Stanley's softening-athlete frame engulfed his chair; both he and his baseball bat sized walking stick leaned against the wall.

At the corner of the table in black cargo pants, a heavy black wool sweater, and black stocking cap – resembling a commando from every 1960's World War II movie ever made – was Jimmy's garage manager, Stick. Stick's history is nearly as sketchy as Nik's. He moved to the U.S. from Canada – most likely illegally, is perpetually pissed-off, and is a mechanic savant. Nik sat on Stick's left and appeared to be dozing.

Both Nik and Stick sat in front of the wall of windows facing 13th Street. I expected a common immigrant with uncommon skills and a sketchy gangland mechanic would avoid windows but they always seemed at ease there. That probably had to do with something I'd noticed long ago: the windows in that corner of the room distorted the view considerably. Not like looking through wavy glass you usually see in a hundred-year-old building, though; more like the view through the abnormally thick laminated glass in a bank drive-thru lane – or Nik's cab and Stanley's missing Escalade.

Stanley and Stick looked beyond furious. In contrast, Jimmy's face was his typical high-stakes poker neutral. I reconsidered asking Rex for a beer — I looked over to him and saw that he was swearing silently at the wine glass he was washing. Probably cursing it for daring to have lipstick on the rim. Once again, I decided to pass on the breakfast brew order.

I sighed and walked toward their table feeling like a fly approaching an airplane's windshield. Stanley's expression darkened with each step I took. When I reached them, he dropped the front legs of his chair onto the floor and reached for his club, er, walking stick.

A dark vehicle slid to a stop at the curb outside of the windows behind Nik and Stick. Even through the funky bullet resistant glass I could see it was a black Escalade. A hulking man in indigo jeans and a black leather biker jacket jumped out of it and ran to the bar's back entrance. He emerged from the doorway next to Jimmy a few moments later. Nik never raised his head from his nap but I noticed his right hand slipped inside his coat.

The driver startled the bejeesups out of me by throwing the truck's key fob into my chest from the doorway. It bounced off my coat and dropped to the floor. As I plucked the fob from the dingy floor tile, the tosser slipped back out the door. A black pick-up truck rolled up behind the Escalade, pausing just long enough for him to hop inside. It sped away before I was upright again.

I looked at Jimmy. I looked at the key fob. Then I looked past Stick and Nik at the Escalade outside. I shook my head at Nik. That crafty old fart had me doubt my own intuition.

"Ha. And ha," I said to the group. "You guys were just messin' with me. I knew it had to be one of Stick's guys who took Stan's truck. I gotta admit, this was one hell of a prank to pull on someone so early in the morning."

I was smiling. No one else was. Not even the hint of a smirk. My grin faltered. And my aching knee trembled.

"Hook, you moron," Stanley growled, "That's a different truck. Now shut up and sit down."

Dammit.

Chapter Four

I dropped into an empty chair facing Jimmy and Stanley. My backside was exposed to the main entrance and the entire barroom highlighting my position on the company org chart. I hoped the buffalo head had my back because I knew Rex sure as hell didn't.

Stick sat with his elbows on the table, his chin resting on his fists. He scowled at me. That was nothing new – the surly Canuck always scowled at me. His garage is downwind from a sewer plant which partly explains his perpetually shitty mood.

Nik's chin rested on his chest, his eyes still closed...and his right hand still inside his jacket. My finely-honed intuition told me he probably wasn't really dozing.

Stanley dropped the front legs of his chair back to the floor with a thud that shook dust motes from the light fixtures. He glared at me like I'd lost his favorite toy. Oh, yeah, I kinda did. I could see all the good will I'd earned saving his life was pretty much gone. I wondered which of my vital organs he would threaten to harvest first.

He gulped a large chunk of air and shook a massive finger at me. He started to speak; Jimmy stopped him with a hand on his shoulder. Stanley clenched his jaw and gripped the tabletop; his glare still smoldered.

Jimmy looked me in the eyes. In the preopening gloom of Bill's his normally pale blue irises were indistinguishable from his pupils. That made sitting across from the most powerful man in Kansas City even more intimidating.

Some of Bill's regulars say Jimmy inherited a "very lucrative family business." Many of them even shamelessly brown-nose when he's in the bar, hoping for a crumb of a handout. All of them were convinced he had several rivals permanently resting at the bottom of the Missouri River. The police are divided in their opinions. Many see Jimmy as an ally, a quiet supporter of the city. Others on the force are convinced he's the metro's top organized crime kingpin and look for any reason to take him down. He does always seem to be on the periphery of major events – both good and bad. Just the same, I believe he's probably an eccentric philanthropist – but I usually do my best not to cross him. Even though my time as his lackey was short and I'd never seen anything remotely resembling a Scorcese film, I still kept my eyes down and ears closed. If Jimmy really was a concrete overshoe salesman I preferred not to be a customer.

Without breaking his stare, he spoke. "How did you manage to lose a company truck?"

"Lose a truck? It was fucking stolen!" I screamed in my head. Out loud, however, I said, "Look, um, Jimmy...guys...it's not my-"

"Fault," Jimmy said, finishing my excuse. "Yeah, it's not your fault."

Jimmy's a powerful man, but he's also extremely smart. I

knew he'd understand.

"Once again, it's not your fault," he said with a heavy sigh.

Oh, crap.

The frosty bar suddenly felt very hot. Beads of sweat trickled down my back like someone'd dumped a bucket of ice down my shirt.

"The Castillo's Lexus wrapped around a power pole – not your fault. Handz Middlebrook's Corvette required so much bodywork it took Stick's guys a month to repair it – not your fault. Your tow truck reduced to a pile of smoldering ash – not your fault. You even managed to disable my own father's Chrysler – again, not your fault. Now, you've lost Stanley's truck."

"That's a bunch of bullshit and you know it," is what my brain shouted.

I looked at my feet and decided they looked better in old leather boots than new concrete overshoes.

"But, um, Jimmy, you know those were all, um, weird circumstances. Hell, you were with me when most of them happened. It really isn't my fault."

He kept his eyes locked on mine. I think five minutes passed since he last blinked.

"No, not your fault. But that is your luck, isn't it?" he asked. He took a drink then continued. "Your back-handed good luck is bad for my business."

I winced. I'd never heard of "back-handed good luck" but I caught the gist. Heck, anyone who knows me could figure out the meaning. Stupid things happen to me. A lot. Broken things. Hurt things. Lost things. Stolen things. Inexplicably goofy things. But, I always end up fine. Sometimes a bit banged up, but otherwise fine. I'm lucky that way. Apparently, back-handed lucky.

"Right," I mumbled. "I'm, uh, sorry, sir."

Stick snickered at my use of the word "sir." Jimmy shot him a look that sobered him up.

"Anyway, while Stick tries to recover the truck, I have a different assignment for you. This is important so try not to luck it up."

The brain trust chuckled at his remark. I didn't care; I wasn't fired. And, honestly, I was bored with delivering papers to and from all of Jimmy's little companies. Jimmy's empire was huge – much larger than I or even the cops knew – and it had a lot of redundancy and inefficiencies. I'd tried many times to point this out to Stanley but he dismissed my observations as "delivery-boy oversimplifications" and that I should "shut the hell up." I was more than ready for something new. Something "important."

"Take the truck," Jimmy said nodding at the Escalade outside, "and go here." He slid a cocktail napkin across the table. Written in sharp block letters was "1524 Main - 5pm."

"5? But I had plans..." I stammered.

The frown on Jimmy's face strongly suggested any plans I had weren't of any consequence to him so I didn't tell him about my date with Dea.

"Butch will tell you what to do when you get there."

"Butch?"

"Yeah, he's a new guy on Stick's crew. Don't piss him off."

Super. One lost Escalade and I was unceremoniously demoted to the point of taking orders from a wrench-turning knuckle dragger.

I waited a few seconds for more instructions. All I got were stares and the puffs of condensation from everyone's breathing.

"All right, then," I said, sliding my chair back. I stood and turned to the front door.

"Hook," Stanley said, "be careful."

I warmed a little. Deep down I knew Stan and I were still buds.

Then he clarified. "Be careful with my new ride. Try not to lose this one, too."

Everyone at the table laughed – Jimmy included this time. I reddened and walked out of the bar. As I limped past the windows along 13th on my way to the SUV I saw the shadow of Rex taking a tray of drinks to Jimmy's table. The grouchy prick probably turned up the thermostat after I left, too.

I pulled myself into the truck. It still smelled of fresh Scotchgard. Stick's guys hadn't even installed the security keypad yet. I pressed the ignition button and started it. Some say the growl of a brand-new truck is no different from the sound of an old beater. Perhaps. It's sounds pretty sweet to me though. I eased onto 13th Street and headed back to my loft.

Chapter Five

Winter thunderstorms are pretty rare in my town so I felt confident lightning wouldn't strike twice. I parked the new Escalade in the open spot: the spot vacated by Stanley's stolen truck. I locked the door to deter amateur thieves and limped to my building.

I bumped into Mrs. Sweeney in the lobby. And I mean I literally bumped into Mrs. Sweeney. I was looking at my feet, wishing my knee didn't feel like a railroad spike was driven into it. She was checking her mailbox near the front door and probably peeking into other peoples' boxes as well. I stepped through the entryway and bounced off her bathrobe-covered plumpness like a pebble off a beachball. My keister ended up on the floor along with an armful of her Hollywood gossip magazines and Franklin Mint collectible spoon catalogs.

She gave me a venomous glare as I hastily gathered her third-class mail.

"Sorry, Mrs. Sweeney. I, um, didn't see you there."

Her comically tiny head tilted down at the terrycloth housecoat she wore, its size likely had same number of exes as the actress on the cover of one of her magazines. I sheepishly handed back her mail.

"And I don't see you," she said with her squeaky voice, "with my precious Dea."

I rolled my eyes in reply but she also didn't see that; she'd already wobbled away.

I pushed myself onto my feet. My knee ached even more from my most recent tumble. Even so, I managed to limp my ass to the elevator before it arrived for Mrs. Sweeney. We waited in uncomfortable silence until the ancient conveyance's bell clunked. We continued not talking on the slow ascent to the 2nd floor. Mrs. Sweeney gave me a final disapproving look then toted her reading material out of the elevator. As the doors creaked to a close, I swear I heard her mutter "tool."

I made it to my floor without any additional drama. I keyed into my loft expecting to see Patch waiting for me at the door. He was asleep on my couch. His ears twitched slightly to acknowledge my presence when I shut the door.

I walked into the kitchen to check Patch's food and water situation. There was still some food but the bottom of the bowl was partially visible. In a cat's world this indicates starvation is imminent so I added some more kibble and replaced his water, too.

I glanced at the clock on my microwave and sighed. It wasn't even 9 a.m. but my knee throbbed. I pawed through the junk drawer and found the leftover painkillers from my last hospital visit. I shook out thee tablets, added four Advil caplets, and washed them all down with some water.

Patch stood up on the couch and stretched, reaching out with

his front paws as though he was doing some feline form of yoga. He moved to a different cushion, recurled into a perfect circle of gray fur, and resumed sleeping. That seemed like a pretty good idea.

I crossed the room and dropped onto the couch next to him. Down feathers blasted out of the two bullet holes in the back of the sofa (don't ask – that's a whole different story) reminding me I needed to buy a new couch before all the stuffing was gone. I let my eyes drop shut for a few minutes. Six hours later I awoke to Patch standing on my chest.

"Meow."

"Aw, shit, not again," I replied.

I hobbled over to a window and looked down to the parking lot. The new truck was right where I left it. The little furball was messing with me.

"Really, Patch?"

He walked into the kitchen and sat down in front of the pantry. He looked at the cabinet door. He looked at me and blinked. All the little con artist wanted was a treat. I opened the Kitty Krak jar and dropped a couple of treats in front of him. He wolfed down his nuggets and then sprinted back to the coffee table in front of the sofa. He leapt onto it and pawed at my personal cell phone.

The phone dinged, announcing a text message.

I crossed the room and picked up the phone. The message was from Dea. Naturally. Much like only Stanley calls me on the Jimmy Phone, only Dea calls my personal phone. When I started working for Jimmy pretty much everyone else I knew stopped contacting me.

Dea was still working at her coffee shop. Her employee called in sick with a tattoo and body piercing emergency. She was alone until close and swamped with hipster millennials on holiday break. I texted back to her that I was doing a thing for Jimmy and would call her later.

The clock on my seldom-used oven said I still had over an hour before I needed to leave. My growling stomach suggested I needed to eat. Patch pawing at his nose told me I needed a shower. It crossed my mind I have lots of needs in my life.

I grabbed a bottle of beer and a greasy delivery box from the refrigerator. The two slices of pizza weren't covered in green fuzz but were obviously nearing puberty. I didn't see anything fresher in the 'fridge so I ate the cold wedges of stale carbohydrates. I immediately regretted not eating a piece of the box instead. I washed away the bad taste with the beer on my way to the bathroom. I showered with double the usual amount of Old Spice bath gel to appease Patch's sensitive nose.

Assuming Jimmy wasn't sending me to a dinner party, I threw on my usual blue jeans and old Chiefs sweatshirt. Patch waited for me in the kitchen, staring at the pantry. I knuckled under and gave him another treat then topped-off his food and water. By my oven-sized clock, I still had half an hour before I had to meet Stick's guy.

I looked at Patch. He looked at me then sprinted away, leaping onto the coffee table then to the couch. He was asleep as soon as his head hit the cushions.

Rather than bump around the loft for another 30 minutes I decided to leave early. I pulled on my boots and jacket and headed outside. I slipped out of the building without any run-ins with the gossip girls. To my relief, the truck was still in the lot.

I slip-slided over the frosty and mostly empty streets to Main Street. When I stopped at 15th I was surprised to find the whole block surrounded by a temporary construction fence. The electric streetcar service recently resumed using the rails embedded in Main Street so I avoided that street like the plague; I hadn't been on it in weeks. The two old office buildings I remembered standing there were gone. The remains of a narrow, brick building I didn't recall stood alone in the middle of the block. The fence had sheets of plywood and large "Keep Out" placards attached to it which obscured my view but that didn't explain why a tiny, obviously quite old building stood where I swore only two much larger office buildings used to be. Yet, it looked familiar.

I sat at the wheel staring at it for a couple of minutes before I placed it. The building was the same one I'd seen on the news where Jimmy and his group were interviewed. It must have been wedged in between the other two buildings and escaped my typically razor-sharp attention to detail.

The small structure was in the late stages of being demolished. The upper stories were already gone; all that remained was the ground floor.

I parked near the curb in front of the building entrance. After shutting off the engine I hit the door unlock button and reached for the door handle. For an instant, my hand was paralyzed by a sharp double piercing sensation in my arm. It was like someone was stapling my shirt sleeve to my wrist. Or, more accurately, a one-eyed cat nipping at me as a warning. But, I didn't see anything dangerous.

I swung the door open, breaching the superlative soundproofing the car manufacturer touts in its commercials. Loud humming and clacking sounds filled the cabin of the luxury SUV. Then the door was ripped from my grip.

I recoiled my hand back inside and watched as one of the electric streetcars whizzed past. The truck door clattered up the street and came to rest in the gutter about 50 feet in front of me. Once the train was clear, it blew its horn.

Asshole. The conductor was probably a reassigned Metro bus driver.

I unbuckled and stepped out of the gaping hole that was formerly covered by the door laying in the gutter. I walked up the street and lugged the door back to the truck, tossing it into the back seat. Stanley was going to be displeased. Very displeased. I sighed and headed for the building.

I slipped through the fence gate. Two deep, building-sized holes flanked the remaining structure. My keen powers of observation told me the buildings I remembered had already been demolished.

Staying well clear of the holes, I carefully stepped around the sheet of plywood blocking the building entrance. A bare bulb dangled from the ceiling casting harsh shadows in the debris filled lobby. A couple of small rooms were off to my left; gold numbers stenciled on their transom windows above the doorways hinted they were probably dreary offices at one time. The yellowed walls were trimmed with dark, battered molding. Everything else, carpeting, furniture – even the doors – had been removed. I walked into the closest office, accidentally kicking an empty five-gallon bucket across the room. The racket echoed throughout the room and lobby. I froze until the sound died. No one came to investigate.

An open stairway with ornate, iron balusters and a thick oak railing filled the end of the lobby. A rusty-beige, steel folding chair stood guard in front of it. A section of orange plastic snow fence duct taped to the balusters half-assed blocked off the stairs going up to the missing floors.

Beside the stairway to nowhere was a jagged opening in the old plaster-and-lath wall. Inside the opening was a battered steel door. It creaked open. A bear-sized man in denim coveralls and a black leather jacket covered with club badges stepped out. He looked like the kind of guy who seasons his fries by putting his face over the plate and tapping the end of his nose. The door clunked shut behind him.

My finely-honed powers of deduction told me this was Stick's guy.

"Hey, Butch."

"You're early, ya foockin' chirp," he growled with a heavy north-of-the-border accent.

Yep, definitely one of Stick's guys.

I figured this was a shitty assignment – Stanley's way of punishing me for losing his truck. I had no clue how Butch got stuck with the same gig. He should have been happy I was early. But, Stick's guys were never happy to see me.

I shrugged.

He glared at my indifference. He pointed to the folding chair and said, "Sit."

"Sit?"

"Sit. And don't let noobody in. Doon't use the bathroom either, ay – it doon't work no more. Port-O-Shitter's outside."

I frowned at the thought of a construction site "toilet" in December.

"And stay oot of the basement," he said in a way that sounded like going into the basement was an unquestionably bad idea.

"Why?" I asked.

He glared at me.

"Because...doon't," he said matter-of-factly.

It occurred to me that not only had I been demoted to unarmed security guard, I was also taking orders from a pit crew reject. I decided my part of the company org chart resides on a square of Charmin – the last square – the one that sticks to the cardboard tube and isn't really useful to anyone.

"Someone will be here in the morning to replace you."

Wait – did he say "morning?"

"Morning?" I asked.

He glared some more.

"Just gimme the truck key, ay."

Key? Why did he want the key? Stick's guys all rode large and obnoxiously loud motorcycles. I panicked. The last time I spent the night stranded in a crummy old building didn't go very well. Plus, there was just over a hundred percent chance he'd notice the driver's door was missing and I still hadn't yet noodled out a believable story to explain it.

"What? Key? Don't you have a bike?"

He rolled his eyes and glanced out a window. Although a thick sheet of opaque plastic replaced the glass, the snow covering the construction equipment was obvious even to me.

"Oh, um, yeah," I said, reluctantly tossing him the key fob for the truck. "It isn't locked. And, be careful with it – it's brand-new."

He walked through my shoulder like I was the door to an old west saloon. A few seconds later I heard a sharp "what the actual fuck?" I waited for him to come back for an explanation. He must have been aware of my reputation; instead the engine started and then he roared away.

The air in the lobby was dead still. It was so quiet I could hear the crackle of my boogers slowly refreezing. Unsurprisingly, no television was to be seen. There wasn't even the usual construction site radio. I almost wished I had a book. And liked to read. Almost.

Wood sawhorses blocked the doors under the "Restrooms" sign; I reminded myself to think dry thoughts or I'd be forced to use the frozen fiberglass outhouse outside. The bubbling, churning Missouri River immediately sprang into my head. Even though I was borderline dehydrated, I suddenly felt the need to take a leak.

Dammit.

Ignoring my predecessor's orders, I stepped around a sawhorse and peeked into the Men's Room. I was greeted with the view of a large, ceramic-tiled room with galvanized steel pipes poking through the walls above four holes in the floor. The thought of using a frozen Tupperware crapper temporarily drove away my urge to whiz. I turned around and walked back to the center of the lobby.

My phone rang. Without Patch to warn me, it scared the bejeezups out of me. I fumbled through my pocket and pulled out my personal phone. It was Dea. I jabbed at the screen three times before realizing my gloved hand couldn't answer the call. On the fourth ring, I bonked my nose with the screen and hoped for the best.

"Hullo?" I said, half expecting dead air in reply.

"Hook? Where are you? Did you just get slapped?"

"Uh, no, not exactly," I said, my words punctuated by puffs of vapor in the frigid air. "I'm just chillin' in one of Jimmy's buildings."

"I'm almost done at the shop – I can drop by later if you want."

I took a look around the lobby. I ran a gloved fingertip along the stair rail and discovered under the thick layer of construction dust was another, older layer of dust. The little office building I'd never noticed apparently was unnoticed by anyone for many years. I doubted even in its heyday it would have been a fun place for a date.

"Um, nah, that's ok. It's just a cruddy little building that's half demolished," I said. The bare bulb flickered. "I'm not sure how safe it is even."

"What cruddy building?"

"Well, I'm at what's left of 15th and Main. Everything is rubble except–"

"You're at the Library?" she shouted. I jerked the phone away from my ear. I barely heard "I'll be over as soon as I close" before she abruptly hung up on me.

"Library?" I asked the folding chair. Its steely reply indicated to me it didn't know what she meant either.

I shrugged and flopped onto the chair.

Chapter Six

Seconds after I sat down a sharp click followed by a thunderous whooshing sound echoed from behind the steel door. My heart skipped a couple of thumps. It sounded like a cyclone blasting through the basement.

I stayed glued to the folding chair as though it would shield me from danger. Fortunately, the building didn't collapse – at least not immediately. I stood up very carefully lest my movements become the straw that broke the building's support beams; to my relief the floor held. My senses were jarred a second time when the tornado abruptly stopped.

My thoughts shifted from disaster to malice. Someone else had to be in the building. I thought about calling the cops but Jimmy never called them for anything so I figured I probably shouldn't either. There was no point in contacting Stanley; he would just call me a wuss and tell me to deal with it. I sighed and pushed myself off the chair.

A quick scan of the lobby didn't reveal any potential weapons aside from the plastic bucket I'd kicked. I frowned then stepped toward the stairs, mentally preparing myself to use my dukes if confronted. Then I spied a 2-foot section of electrical conduit on the floor below one of the sawhorses. It was about half an inch in diameter and weighed about as much as a Taco Bell spork. But, it was something. I scooped up the makeshift billy club and tiptoed to the door.

I opened it a few inches. The hinges screeched. I stopped. No new sounds came from behind it. I slowly pulled it open enough to slip past, the hinges protesting the whole way. I stepped through the gap and paused on the other side.

Behind it a stairway descended into shadows. Even with my piece of pipe and the flashlight app on my phone, I felt ill-equipped to confront any interlopers. Or any lopers for that matter.

I took another look. The stairway wasn't any lighter. I took a deep breath and carefully stepped into the gloom.

The stairs didn't end in another lobby like I expected. Halfway down I realized I was descending into a large office. I paused and checked out the room. A floodlight beside the stairway cast a harsh, halogen-yellow pallor over much of the space. The walls skulking in the work light's shadows, appeared to be covered with bookshelves. A small chandelier hung from the center of the ceiling and was, of course, unlit. A round walnut table was centered below the chandelier.

I saw hints of maroon carpeting on the floor although most of it was under large sheets of cardboard. The spotlight's focus was a large, oak executive desk in the corner of the room, paired with a leather high-backed chair positioned behind it to face the stairs.

A built-in dry bar near the desk, unfortunately, looked totally dry. Despite the commotion I heard from the lobby, I didn't see anyone.

I took a few more steps. The distinctive dry snap of arcing electricity rang out from beside the stairs startling me mid-step.

I've heard that sound way too many times. Out of habit, I shouted "Stungun!" to no one in particular then promptly caught the heel of my boot on the nosing of the stair. My toe dove into the next tread, wrenching my ankle and jarring my bad knee. I yelped in pain then tumbled down the last three steps. The makeshift conduit club flipped out of my hand, rolled across the cardboard, and came to a rest under the desk. I thudded onto the floor as a new tornado blasted through the room.

"Uhnff."

A Saharan gale blew up my pant legs toasting my testes. I looked over my shoulder, directly into the large, orange eye of an industrial grade, forced-air propane heater. I felt achingly stupid; those noisy things are quite common on construction sites. The heater's thermostat clicked again and the heater shut down.

I clutched the newel post and pulled myself onto my feet. My knee throbbed from the misstep and my ribs ached from my belly flop onto the floor. At least the room was warm.

The not-so-baffling mystery was solved but I felt a little conflicted. When Stick's gorilla told me to stay in the lobby, I assumed it was to watch the doors. That didn't seem to apply to him, though, and the blatant double standard really torqued me off. I looked at the stairs; my knee and ankle said I could stay in the office for a little while. I hobbled over to the chair and dropped into it.

I fished a small pill bottle from my front jeans pocket, a constant companion since I first banged up my knee. After dry swallowing a few Advil, I slouched into the crunchy old leather chair.

The room was warm. Stiflingly warm. The dry, propane-fueled heat had to be bad for the wood covered walls but I guessed proper humidity wasn't much of a concern in a building being demolished. My eyes began to droop from the über-strength Advil and the overly warm room.

As my brain slowly faded into nappy time, my subconscious tumbled through my surroundings. The upper floors were gone. The lobby was stripped of everything, including doors. Even the sinks and toilets were gone. Something didn't jive. My eyelids sprang open.

This room...this room was still furnished. The carpeting was even protected from damage. "So, why the hell are you still down here?" I asked the seemingly superfluous desk.

It refused to answer. Stubborn bastard.

The news report Patch made me watch mentioned a "mystery." The only thing mysterious to me was why a partly preserved office was in the basement of a mostly demolished building.

I spun around in the chair, taking in the room. The chair stopped swiveling when my good knee banged into the knob of a desk drawer. The ancient desk shook and it hurt like hell. I reached for my leg to knead away the pain. I felt a sharp, piercing pain in the top of my hand. I didn't know why Patch was warning me but I didn't have another truck door to sacrifice to find out. I dropped to the floor and curled up under the desk for protection. To further make myself invincible, I closed my eyes and held my breath.

Several seconds passed. Then several more. Nothing happened. Just to be sure, I played roadkill for a few more seconds until I couldn't hold my breath any longer. Gasping for air, I slowly opened my eyes.

Blood oozed from a gash on my hand. I sat up to get a better look and was jarred by another sharp pain, this time in the top of the head. I flinched and was rewarded with another jab in my dome. No blood ran through my hair so I ducked and crawled out from my hidey-hole.

A thin wood panel dangled from the bottom of the desk. I shrewdly deduced the tiny metal nail in the corner of the panel was the cause of the gash in my hand. And the pain in my noggin.

Son of a bitch if my knee didn't break the old desk. Between the truck door and the desk I had a feeling Jimmy wasn't giving me an end-of-year bonus. I gently pushed the panel back into place. It held for an instant then dropped loose again. This time a small object fell to the floor.

I looked down at a key. A strange looking tarnished brass key with a triangular shaft. I picked it up. For a moment, I considered stuffing it back into its cubbyhole. However, curiosity got the better of me. I figured I had several hours to kill, so why not explore a little and see where the key fit?

Who wouldn't?

In retrospect, I should have just lodged the key back into the desk and gone back to my cold metal chair in the lobby.

Chapter Seven

Since I was already on the floor I figured I may as well check out the rest of the antique behemoth. I tapped around the creaky old desk like a sawbones checking someone's reflexes.

How I jarred open the key compartment so easily became very apparent: the hot, dry air was destroying the massive beauty, which was a damn shame. The joints were loose, the unexposed panels shrank, and a few other visible finish nails popped loose. The desk's value fell a little more every time the heater ignited.

There weren't any other secret spaces under the desk – at least none I would ever discover. I felt around inside the key compartment but found nothing more. I tacked the key's panel back into place with the original brad and hoped it would hold long enough to make it someone else's problem. I grabbed my conduit baton and hoisted myself back into the chair.

Every drawer had a keyhole on its face. The old piece's worth was further diminished by the half-assed job someone did of prying them all open. Not that it mattered to me – the key didn't fit any of them anyway. I went through them just the same and found a couple of rusty paperclips, an empty manila folder, and a #2 pencil that looked like it was sharpened with a pocket knife.

I backed the chair away from the desk and spun back and forth in it a few times. According to the clock on my phone, Dea's arrival was at least 20 minutes away. I looked at the odd key again and decided to expand my exploration.

I rolled the chair backward and to the left a few feet to the dry bar, slightly ashamed of myself for not checking out the booze situation first. Naturally, the dusty decanters on the marble countertop were bone-dry – not a surprise since Stick's goons guarded the place. The key didn't fit the lock on the liquor cabinet but, just like the desk, it didn't matter: the cabinet doors had been pried open. I looked inside; there were no secret compartments. A lone, empty Old Harper bottle stood silent watch in the back corner.

I pushed myself out of the chair and moved toward the nearest wall to look for more cabinets. All I found were book-laden shelving. There were old leather-bound editions of stuff I recognized and a lot of stuff I didn't: *The Adventures of Tom Sawyer, 20,000 Leagues Under the Sea, Black Beauty*, three *Oliver Twist*s – even *The Book of Mormon* and something I couldn't understand, *Война и мир*. The room was stocked like a high school librarian's torture chamber.

The cast from the work light faded pretty quickly the further I got from the desk and bar. A few steps into the inky shadows my feet discovered a small pile of books. I stumbled, falling into another set of shelves. I dropped the pipe and grasped for anything to keep me upright. I knocked several more books onto the floor before finally falling on top of them.

"Ooonph."

I was positive I cracked a testicle. I rolled onto my back and discovered the pain was actually an old Bible on the top of the pile digging into my privates. I groaned. Through the gloom, I watched a couple more books slowly teeter on a shelf above me. They seemed to magically grow before my eyes. I realized after they bounced off my forehead that gravity was the only magic involved.

I groaned again, only a little louder.

After a few moments of achy contemplation, my curiosity vanished. As boring as it may have been, the uncomfortable folding chair in the main lobby took on a safe appeal.

I pushed myself onto my knees and stopped to wait for the dancing fireflies to clear from my vision. I reached over to the shelf closest to me and pushed on it to help raise myself from the floor. Once again upright – sore but standing – I leaned on the shelf to rest a moment. The shelf and part of the wall behind it broke free, crashing to the floor.

"Damn it!"

The renegade shelving ignored my swearing. The building was being demolished so I knew the damaged shelf shouldn't be a big deal. But, the gorilla's instructions to "stay oot of the basement, ay" rang in my head and I was worried some control freak of a demolition worker would get pissed off I'd pre-wrecked part of the room. I picked up the oak shelf and thin paneling attached to it and maneuvered it toward the hole I'd created. As I tried to wedge it back into place, I caught a glimpse of something metallic in the freshly exposed wall.

It was too dark to make out what it was. Curiosity shoved aside my resolve to go back upstairs. I limped back to the work light and aimed it at the shelves. As I neared the wall, the source of the metallic glint became obvious. It was a small wooden knob with a heavily patinaed lock faceplate in the center of it – a lock requiring a triangular shaped key.

The heater's igniter snicked again. I jumped and bounced my head off the bottom of a shelf as a blast of hot air roared through the room. Grumbling at myself for being such an overreacting weenie, I returned my attention to the hole in the wall.

I expected to see concrete or concrete blocks with wood furring behind the paneling, or the usual guts of a basement wall. Instead, there were broad oak planks less than an inch behind the room's paneling. The chunk of shelf I'd pulled from the wall didn't look broken; it was built to be removed.

I looked more closely at the wall and bookshelves around the hole. A barely visible seam in the paneling's molding outlined a door-sized rectangle in the wall. If not for the shrinkage caused by the propane dragon in the room, the outline would have been impossible to see.

I briefly toyed with calling Stanley. Briefly. But he was pretty explicit the last time I phoned him with a question that unless I was in the hospital again to leave him alone.

I glanced at my wrist. It reminded me that Patch had knocked my watch under the bed. Dea was probably still in the middle of closing her shop. Being an obsessive history nut, a secret door in a creepy old basement office seemed like the kind of thing she might find intriguing. However, the fiasco with Al Capone's embarrassingly empty vault flickered in my noggin; I decided to check out things myself first.

The heater clicked off as I peered into the hole in the wall. There were no markings or anything other clues to what was locked away, just the knob with the odd keyhole in its center.

I shrugged. With a big inhale I reached in and inserted the key. As I suspected, the key fit the lock perfectly. I smiled and gave it a twist. It didn't budge.

"What the hell?"

I gave another twist. Still nothing.

I stepped back and stared at the nonfunctioning lock and key. The snick of arcing electricity crackled behind me. The sensation of four kitty fangs clamping onto my ankle dropped me to my knees. I didn't know what was behind the secret door but it was obvious my fuzzy little guardian angel didn't want me to find out.

Then I realized the furnace igniter was still crackling but no blast of hot air followed. I panicked at the thought of propane flooding the room before the faulty starter blew me to many, many small pieces-parts. I whipped my head around to see what was wrong. I found myself looking up at a large figure outfitted like a cold weather Ninja, dressed in black insulated pants and jacket with a full-face ski mask covering his head. What really grabbed my attention, though, was the NeuralScrambler 900 stun gun he held.

Bright blue electricity danced between the two electrodes. I shuddered at the sight of it. I've been zapped with those things so many times I sometimes accidentally jumpstart cars just by walking past them. He waved the little zapper in front of my face. Another, smaller arctic Ninja with a heavy sledge hammer dangling from one hand stepped from behind the first to watch the show.

"Aw shit, man, not a stunner," I pleaded.

He shook a slightly crushed soft pack of Morley's until a rumpled cigarette emerged from the top. Using his lips, he gingerly plucked the unfiltered cancer stick from the pack with the tenderness of kissing an infant on the forehead. He squeezed the stun gun's trigger. I backed into the wall trying to put another few inches between me and my most hated nemesis. The stun gun, I mean; I still had no fucking clue who the ski-masked assholes were. He raised the stun gun to his face, sparking the cig to life with the raw 900,000 volts of electricity arcing between the zapper's electrodes.

Then he waved the crackling 'scrambler near my cheek. Just before I was jolted with high voltage, the small Ninja stepped forward and tagged me on the temple with a solid left jab. Hard. I dropped the floor like a slice of bread buttered on both sides.

Chapter Eight

CLANG

Everything was dark and my head pounded like a blacksmith convention at a hammer factory.

CLANG CLANG CLANG

I realized my eyes were closed. That explained the whole darkness thing.

CLANG CLANG

My head throbbed but the clanging was outside my ears, not in between them. I opened my eyes slowly – and looked straight into an ethereal glow surrounding the long hair and bearded face of Jesus himself.

"Oh, fuck, I've died," I blurted, followed quickly by, "Shit, I just swore at Jesus."

My pottymouth was out of control. Understandably, he scowled. He put a finger to his lips and silently shushed me. I clamped a hand over my mouth before I said another damn word.

Jesus shifted to his left and looked over his shoulder. His glow disappeared. I panicked, afraid I was about to begin a very fiery descent into an eternity of being forced to watch reality TV show reruns.

CLANG

I squinted and realized I was still in the basement office. The hidden door I'd accidentally discovered was open. The dim light streaming through it was the source of Jesus' saintly shimmer.

Jesus focused on the secret door. A loose ponytail dangled down the back of the ragged, olive drab Army jacket he wore. He glanced back at me while reaching into a pocket of his cargo pants.

He gripped my arm like a starving anaconda on a hamster.

"Keep quiet," he hissed then snapped onto my wrist the set of handcuffs he'd surreptitiously pulled from his pocket. I felt around the floor with my free hand and found my club. I swung and hit Jesus in the shoulder. It bent harmlessly around his jacket. He shrugged it away then flipped me onto my stomach, knocking the wind out of me. He finished the cuffing with a speed and efficiency never demonstrated by any cop I'd ever known. Even quicker than my ex-girlfriend, Samantha.

He pushed himself onto his feet by shoving my face into a cracked leather book cover. Judging by its smell, the book had spent somewhere between a thousand and a bajillion years in some grandmother's root cellar.

CLANG CLANG

The sound came through the doorway. I had a view of the secret door but my floor level vantage point didn't give me a view of what lay beyond it.

"Don't move and you won't get hurt," he whispered.

Despite being cloaked in the bulky field jacket and cargo pants, Jesus was obviously built more like a corner back in the NFL than a carpenter from Nazareth. The religious icon glided silently to the opening like a lion looking for Daniel.

He paused at the edge of the doorway for a few moments, peering inside. He reached into a pants pocket again.

CLANG

He waited for a second CLANG then slipped through the doorway during the noise.

CLANG

A lighter clank echoed dully from the room. I heard grunts and the shuffling of a scuffle. Someone shouted, "STOP!" A different voice yelled, "GO!" An instant later, the ninja thugs burst through the doorway and leapt over me. I heard their boots pound up the stairway behind me.

I tried to roll over to make sure they were completely gone. I regretted the move immediately. From the corner of my eye I saw Jesus sprint through the doorway. He jumped just as I flopped onto my side. He kicked me in the back with both his hiking boots and crashed to the floor.

He pushed himself onto all fours and glared at me.

"I told you DON'T MOVE!"

Then Jesus knocked me unconscious with a wicked right hook to my jaw.

Chapter Nine

The world was shaking and dark – like a bouncy castle during a massive midnight earthquake. My head throbbed.

A muffled woman's voice called to me, "Hook?"

The earth kept shaking – and it was talking to me.

"Hook! Wake up!" the female voice said again, but more clearly.

The fog in my brain thinned slightly. I remembered something very important: open eyes.

I opened my eyes and the darkness disappeared; a freakin' miracle I tells ya. However, the earthquake continued. The dingy maroon and gilt cover of Poe's *The Raven* stared at me and I felt a small pool of saliva against my cheek – both good signs I was still in the basement office, albeit face down on the cardboard covered floor.

My head hurt like...well, like two assholes had punched me in the head. At least the blacksmith stopped his annoying clanging. The quaking resumed.

"Hook!" a woman shouted while my world trembled.

Not just any woman, though. My head finally cleared enough for me to recognize Dea's voice. Eager to see a friendly face, I flipped onto my back. I saw her cute freckles and beautiful hazel eyes looking down on me and shouted, "Ow! Son of a bitch!" as the high strength steel bracelets I wore gouged painfully into my wrists and back. I twisted which only increased the pain; I surrendered my man-card with a high-pitched yelp. Dea let go of my shoulders and knelt beside me. She grabbed the collar of my jacket and helped me sit up.

"Hook, what's going on?"

Glancing around the room filled with smelly old books and a secret door, I struggled with where to begin and how much to say. My brain tumbled through recent events but an easy synopsis escaped me.

"It's...it's a, uh, long story," I deflected. The pain in my wrists reminded me of a more immediate concern.

"Can you, um, help me with these cuffs?"

Footsteps on the stairway interrupted my stalling.

"Oh, shit," I said, "He's back!"

We whipped our heads to the stairway. But it was neither the winter ninjas nor the mercenary deity. It was Jimmy. Pausing midway down, he looked around the room and pursed his lips. He finished his descent and crossed the room, stopping beside Dea. My boss looked down on me with a combination of confusion and disdainful pity.

"Hook, what the hell's going on?"

"Really, it's kind of a long story," I answered.

"It usually is with you," he said with a sigh. "Humor me."

"Well, I, uh, heard a noise down here. So, I came down to see what it was."

I gulped some air, frantically trying to think of a delicate way to tell Jimmy I broke the antique desk. Nothing came to mind. So, I skipped that detail altogether.

"I was looking around the room when I got jumped by two huge guys in ski masks. One of them tried to taze me then the, er-" I paused. No one really needed to know the small one took me down with one punch, right? "-er, the other one knocked me out."

The room was merely uncomfortably warm when it was just a propane heater, the halogen work light, and me in it. The addition of Jimmy grilling me made the space unbearably hot. I wiped some sweat from my forehead with my shoulder, then continued.

"I don't know how long I was out. When I came to, a longhaired, bearded jerk handcuffed me then went after the first two through that door."

Jimmy looked skeptical.

"They ran out and up the stairs. He tried to follow but, uh, tripped over me. Then he punched me. That's the last thing I remember before Dea woke me up."

Dea's eyes were wide.

"Hot Jesus knocked you out?" Dea blurted.

"Hot Jesus?" Jimmy asked.

"Hot Jesus?" I repeated.

She turned crimson.

"Um, well yeah. When I got here, a hot guy with long hair and a beard ran through the foyer. He told me to go downstairs and help my boyfriend." She looked at her feet. "That was pretty er, hot – in a nice the way, I mean, how he cared that Hook was ok, right?" she stammered.

Jimmy smirked at her lame cover for the nickname. I wasn't feeling it either, beings how the bearded asshole knocked me unconscious and stuff.

Sensing the jealousy monster climbing into my head, she changed gears.

"He isn't one of your guys?" she asked Jimmy.

Jimmy cocked his head and frowned.

"No, he doesn't sound like one of mine."

"Great," I said under my breath. "Can I get some help with these cuffs, though?"

Instead of an answer, new footsteps echoed down the stairway. We all turned to see Stanley, still in his tracksuit, lumbering down the stairs. When he got to the last step he stopped and appraised the room much the same as Jimmy had.

"Hook, what the hell did you do? Are those books on the floor? Why are you even down here? And why the hell did you put a heater in here? Are you insane?!"

To accent his question, the heater clicked to life and blasted us with more hot air. Jimmy shot a look at Stanley and shook his head in the direction of the heater. Despite his rebuilt pelvis and knees, Stanley demonstrated his former fullback agility and hopped over the banister to shut off the hot air.

"Hey, this is how I found the place," I protested after the whooshing subsided. Then I added, "Can someone help with these cuffs?"

Jimmy picked up a book from the floor. His brow furrowed. He looked at Stanley and said, "Change of plans. Get the team over here tonight."

While Jimmy was focused on his cryptic conversation with Stanley, Dea backed up a few steps and looked at the secret doorway.

"Um, Jimmy..." she said timidly.

He looked to her, noticing for the first time the secret door. He walked over to the opening but ignored the room beyond it. Instead, he studied the lock for a few moments then twisted the old key and removed it. He held it up for everyone to see.

"Was this where you found it, too?" he asked me with a hint of a frown before dropping it into his pocket.

Chapter Ten

More footfalls on the stairway stopped Jimmy from quizzing me further. A bewildered Sergeant Craig Stevens of the Kansas City Police Department paused near the bottom and, just like Jimmy and Stanley had done, carefully surveyed the room.

Instead of the department's standard dark navy polyester uniform, he wore jeans, a flannel shirt, and an oversized black jacket that we all knew was more for covering his shoulder-holstered pistol than it was for warmth. The KCPD badge clipped to his belt announced he was merely "plain clothes" and not "under cover."

He and I trained together for several months before I was unfairly fired from the force. Unlike most of the other officers I once considered friends, Sergeant Stevens and I remained pretty tight.

"Hook, what the hell did you do this time?"

More "generally tolerant" than "tight," actually.

I sighed.

"Really, it's a long story," I said again.

Most of my faculties had returned. It dawned on me the room was awfully crowded considering I hadn't called anyone. Especially not the cops. I needed to make it clear to Jimmy and Stanley that I didn't call Stevens.

"Why are you even here? Nobody called the cops," I said glancing around the room to make sure Stanley and Jimmy heard me say it.

"A trolley conductor called and said some idiot in an Escalade scratched the front of his train with his door," Stevens replied. "You know anything about that?"

I squirmed uncomfortably. Stanley balled his hands into fists and glared at me.

"You hit a train with my new ride?" Stanley growled.

"Don't be ridiculous," I non-answered.

"So the trolley didn't tear off your truck's door?" Stevens asked.

I dug my heels into the cardboard on the floor and scooted around to defend myself to Stevens and Stanley. "Hey," I said, "the lunatic driving that train sped up to hit me."

"The trains run by computer," Stanley said through clenched teeth.

"So, a conductor called you, too?" I asked.

Stanley rolled his eyes. "Of course not. Jimmy did."

I heel-scooted my butt around again so I could see Jimmy. He shrugged. "Dea called me."

My jaw dropped. My girlfriend had Jimmy's phone number. *I* didn't even have my boss's phone number.

Dea, staring into the secret room again, spoke before I could ask why.

"Jimmy, this is the Library, right?" she asked.

"Dea," I said, "a few books on the floor hardly make it a library."

Jimmy pursed his lips for a moment, shifting his weight from right to left then back to his right again. He glanced at Stanley and a puzzled Sgt. Stevens then contradicted me. "Yes, it is," he replied.

"And that," she said pointing into the secret room, "is the Special Collections?"

I used my heels again to scoot across the floor to the doorway. I followed everyone else's gaze and saw a plain concrete room. Glowing weakly was a single bulb in a gray metal and glass fixture that would have been more at home in a coal mine than a basement. Below the light was an ancient iron safe roughly hobbit tall and two feet square. Climax Saloon was stenciled diagonally across its front in shiny gold script. The winter ninjas' sledgehammer lay on the floor next to it.

Stating the obvious, I said, "So, that's what the clanging sound was."

Jimmy snorted. "That's a Herring & Farrel industrial floor safe. It would take dynamite to crack it."

He paused and scrutinized the main room again. At the end of his appraisal he said, "This room is contaminated enough. Everyone out."

Stanley seemed to understand Jimmy's order – but Dea and Stevens looked shocked at the abrupt command. Me? Heck, I'm used to Jimmy's odd whims so I wasn't fazed at all.

Jimmy's face was hard, conveying that he was serious. Everyone headed toward the stairs. Except me. I still sat on the floor with the Hot Jesus' handcuffs on my wrists.

"Hey, um, guys. Seriously, can someone give me a hand with these cuffs?" I asked while struggling onto my knees.

All four stopped and looked at me like it was the first they knew I was handcuffed. Jimmy and Stanley reached into their front pockets but Dea beat them to the draw. She pulled a key from her purse and walked back to help me. Stevens, the lone person in the room with a legitimate reason to have a key, just shook his head and walked up the stairs.

Chapter Eleven

Stanley and Jimmy climbed the stairs while Dea uncuffed me. When we reached the lobby Stevens had already gone – probably fuming about the report he'd have to make up for the trolley hit-and-run. Jimmy and Stanley talked quietly in the empty front office.

We walked past the folding chair and stood outside the Jimmy-Stanley conference.

"...this'll wreck our news conference," Stanley said, throwing his hands up in frustration.

"Perhaps. But we can't jeopardize the find any more – who knows how bad the damage is?" Jimmy said, waving his hands in reply. It was weird seeing them this flustered about something other than me.

Stanley grunted. "Fine, I'll reschedule to give us a couple more days to-"

"No," Jimmy interrupted, "we'll do it tomorrow." He stopped when he saw Dea and I lingering outside the doorway.

"What?" he snapped at me.

"Did you, um, want me to stay and watch the place?" I asked.

Stanley opened his mouth to answer but the front door spoke

first. The piece of plywood covering the entrance moved aside. Two young men and an older woman stepped through, each pulling a large wheeled tool case. Without saying a word, they walked straight to the metal door we'd just exited and descended the stairs. The sound of their cases thudding down each step echoed through the lobby.

Stan again opened his mouth to answer but a tall, muscular woman in a black uniform cradling a shotgun in her arms and toting a Glock on her hip stepped into the lobby. Her hair was pulled into a bun so tight that her eyebrows migrated into her forehead. She crossed through the room and took up a post next to the metal door.

Stanley shook his head and, nodding at the new guard, said, "No, I think Terra's got it covered." I didn't think it was possible but the Amazonian guard stood even straighter at his words.

Jimmy, using a kinder tone, looked past me to Dea and said, "Make sure he gets home." Then he turned and very curtly said to me "Stanley will have another truck for you in the morning."

Jimmy turned his back on us. He and Stanley resumed their conversation, still very animated but in indecipherably harsh whispers. I leaned in to listen. My finely tuned observational skills detected Stanley's glare. Dea and I quickly left the building right after he told us to "get the fuck out."

Dea's Corolla was parked where I'd left the Escalade – except her driver's door was still attached to the car. We hopped inside. I was barely buckled up when she launched away from the curb.

On a normal day, Dea is an assertive driver. No, actually more aggressive than assertive. Scratch that. She typically drives like a bat out of hell being chased by the devil himself. Her normal days...yeah, those normal days were like a leisurely Country Club Plaza carriage ride compared to this trip. I snuck a glance at my girlfriend to make sure Nik hadn't somehow taken the wheel instead. A couple of minutes later we slid to stop in the loft parking lot.

I waited a few moments for my heart to thump a little slower.

"Are we late for something?" I asked. My fingers ached from clenching the door handle and safety belt.

"What?" she snapped then blushed. "Oh, sorry. Nik's been giving me lessons."

"What? Driving lessons from Nik? When? Wha...why?"

She ignored me. "I'm just excited," she continued. "I didn't think the Library was real."

I shook my head. "Dea, Dea, Dea. Like I said earlier, a few old books laying around didn't make that a library."

She shook her head in frustration. "Not *a* library, we were in *the* Library. The Boss's Library."

She sighed. "Don't you read anything I give you?"

We'd only dated a few times before I discovered Dea's an amateur historian. She has dozens of books on local lore, from architecture to sports to her favorite topic: mobsters. She's given me several to read so I'll have a greater appreciation of my hometown. I, on the other hand, am less enthusiastic about my city's past. But, I've read every book she's given me. Perused them, anyway. Leafed through them, actually. Well, I've memorized their back covers. Most of the back covers. Someday, though, I really do plan to read them. At least the ones that haven't been made into movies.

"Pfff, of course I do," I sputtered. That was a gross over exaggeration of course, but I didn't think she'd like the honest-to-God truth.

The skeptical look on her face didn't even flicker. "The Boss's Library was supposedly neutral ground where all the city bosses would meet to work out disagreements."

I tried to appear interested but I could feel my eyes slowly glaze over.

"I see," I said.

I didn't.

She rolled her eyes at me.

"That place is legendary. And the safe – most of the stuff I've read said the safe was a myth, just a rumor spread to keep the bosses' crews in line."

I had no fuckin' clue what she was talking about. I nodded emphatically in agreement just the same.

"Sure, keep them in line. Because the safe has all that, uh, cash..."

She winced at "cash."

"...er, photographs..."

She scowled.

"...um, secret employment contracts..."

She slugged me in the shoulder.

"I knew you didn't read anything. Nobody knows what's in it for sure, just that it was important enough that the entire city wants what's in it." She leaned closer to me. Her eyes grew wide and she grinned like a teenaged boy stumbling into his first strip club. "Personally, I think it's filled with lists of Black Hand extortion victims."

I shuddered. Mostly because her car was getting chilly, partly because even mentioning the old mob bosses gave me the jeebie-heebies. I know for a fact those dudes hold a grudge.

"That sounds a lot like evidence – only an idiot hangs on to evidence," I said, still shivering.

"The victims were ones who paid: it would be like a list of donors if they ever needed fast cash," she replied while opening her door.

"How do you know the list would only be the ones who paid?" I asked, thinking I'd painted her into a historical corner.

"Duh," she said patronizingly. "The cemeteries have the lists of those who didn't pay. For a tow truck driver, you sure don't know much about leverage."

My jaw dropped at the thought.

"Former tow truck driver!" I weakly protested as she hopped out of the car.

"Former," I stressed again to the empty car. When it didn't answer, I slid out and followed Dea. She practically sprinted to our building. I trotted as quickly as I could to catch up but she easily beat me inside.

Fortunately, Mrs. Sweeney just happened to be in the lobby checking her mail again. It occurred to me that considering the postman only stops at our building once a day, she and Mrs. Crabetts spend an awful lot of time in the lobby checking their mailboxes. She was talking Dea's ear off when I limped through the door.

"...and there's a very handsome young man at my bank. He wears a suit and," she said turning to me, "is very respectable."

I clenched my jaw. Dea wore the same patronizing smile she gives me when I suggest seeing a movie by Alan Smithee.

"Thank you so much for thinking of me," she said sidling toward the elevator, "but I'm in a bit of a rush right now. We can talk more later."

The elevator dinged and the old doors screeched open. Dea boarded. Mrs. Sweeney waddled in behind her. I saw her chubby finger jabbing frantically at the <DOOR CLOSE> button but, as usual, that button did nothing. I slipped between the doors as they closed. The three of us stood uncomfortably as the car creaked upwards. It bumped to a stop on the 2nd floor. Mrs. Sweeney tottered out. "Good night Mrs. Sweeney," I said insincerely. Dea followed her through the doors.

"Uh, wait a second," I stammered. "Aren't you coming up?"

Dea looked at me, her eyes bright with excitement.

"Oh, not tonight," she replied. "I've got way too much research to do now and you don't have the right books." She turned and strode down the hallway. Mrs. Sweeney raised her snout in the air and gave me a very satisfied "hmph" as the doors between us clanked shut.

Chapter Twelve

I opened the door to our loft and found Patch sitting on the floor staring at the doorway. The little guy probably waited impatiently there the whole time I was gone. Or, he sat down in that spot when he heard the elevator doors rattle open.

His whiskers drooped with disappointment when he didn't see Dea. He sprinted to the kitchen and leapt onto the counter, demanding a couple bits of Kitty Krak to console him.

I tossed my jacket onto the floor and fetched his treats from the pantry. After dropping a couple of morsels onto the counter beside him, I grabbed a Cinderblock Pale Ale from the 'fridge. Patch crunched on the treats like a wood chipper gobbling up bowling balls. Without even a thank you meow, he jumped to the floor and scampered into the living room.

I followed and found him sitting on the coffee table. His fuzzy butt rested on one of the books Dea left for me to read. He turned his back to me and pointedly washed a paw.

"Hey, I'm bummed she didn't come up tonight, too," I said.

He stood up and stepped away from the book. He kicked with a back paw a few times until the book flipped onto the floor.

"Yeah, that would probably help."

He winked at me with his good eye then trotted into the bedroom. I tossed my phone and keys onto the coffee table and retrieved the book from the floor. More feathers puffed out of the bullet holes when I flopped onto the couch. I sighed.

For some ambiance, I switched on the TV and flipped to a football game, the commercial-filled Irrelevant Bowl featuring a pair of schools no one other than their alumni ever knew existed. I opened Dea's book and started reading about the Black Hand and its extortion schemes that terrified Kansas City residents in the early 1900s. Somewhere between seeing Mid Central State Tech miss an extra point kick and reading an overly vivid description of a non-paying extortion victim blasted with a sawed-off shotgun, I dozed off.

A fuzzy paw bopped me on the nose, jarring me from my nap. Patch leapt from my chest to the coffee table when I lurched awake.

"Aw, come on, Patch."

I expected him to be more sympathetic considering he sleeps 20 hours a day.

"Can't ya let a guy catch a few minutes of rest?"

In response, Patch pawed at my work phone on the table. The screen lit up displaying "6:42" as the current time. I'd only dozed off for a few minutes.

The television flashed back from the commercial to regular programming. A rerun of *SportsCenter* had replaced the snoozebowl.

Patch stared at the phone. The screen changed to "BLOCKED NAME" as it buzzed for an incoming call. He pawed at the screen, activating the speakerphone function.

"Hook!" Stanley snapped through the phone, "Why are you still sleeping?"

I looked around the room for cameras but dismissed that idea as irrational paranoia. Surely, he just made a lucky guess.

"It's just a nap," I snapped.

"Nap my ass. It's morning. Get dressed and outside. "Your-," he said, breaking up with laughter, "your new ride is waiting." He continued laughing and abruptly hung up.

He only yelled a little – that was nice. My infallible intuition, though, told me the laughter was somehow at my expense.

Stanley didn't give me a deadline so I figured I had time to shower. The jeans and sweatshirt I'd shed smelled faintly of the musty Library – clean enough for another day in my book – so I put them on again.

Patch had returned to his perch on the kitchen counter when I came back out of the bedroom. I added some kibble and fresh water to his bowls. After dropping a piece of Kitty Krak next to him, I grabbed my coat from the floor and headed out the door.

The elevator was blessedly devoid of gossipy neighbors. I shifted from foot to foot as the car rattled toward the ground. Stanley was uncharacteristically late with his follow-up phone call; that made me nervous. I also wondered how many black Escalade SUVs Jimmy had in his company fleet because I was running through them pretty quickly.

The elevator shuddered to a stop at the ground floor. My work phone vibrated. I fumbled it out of my pocket while the doors slid apart. I tapped <ANSWER> and pressed the phone to my ear as I stepped off the elevator – and thudded into the sour mountain of a woman, Mrs. Crabetts.

"Shit," I said reflexively. "I mean damn, er darn. I'm sorry."

Mrs. Crabetts's expression soured further. Stanley's voice crackled in the phone.

"Hook, what the hell are you talking about?" he asked.

"Um-."

"You should be. And watch your language," Mrs. Crabetts snapped.

"Er, yes ma'am," I stammered.

The phone cracked again.

"What'd you call me?"

Stanley was pissed but so was Mrs. Crabetts – and she was right in front of me. The nearest bad attitude took precedence.

"Excuse me, Mrs. Crabetts," I squeaked then rushed for the door.

She stared me down, even gesturing with two fingers from her eyes to me. I half-heartedly waved back with several more fingers than I really wanted to use.

"Hook!" Stanley shouted into my ear, "Quit bickering with Mrs. Crabetts and get outside."

I looked at my phone to see if I'd accidentally enabled a video chat. I hadn't. I began to believe Stanley was an ill-tempered psychic.

I stepped outside. The biting wind drew tears from my eyes,

tears that froze my lashes together. The ice crystals turned my eyes into frozen kaleidoscopes.

The building door slammed behind me. Suddenly, Stanley's laughter echoed into my ear – along with what sounded like Stick and Nik's guffaws.

I rarely hear Stanley laugh, and when I do, it's typically at me.

"Stanley, what the hell?" I asked, scraping away tear-cicles. The laughter continued. When my vision cleared, I saw one of Jimmy's Escalades at the curb, its engine running, and the windows down. Nik and Stick's grinning faces filled the back window. Stanley's monstrous noggin hung out the front window. He pointed past the front of his truck.

"We brought your new ride!" he shouted. Their childish giggles echoed through the phone and over the wind. I turned in the direction of his waggling finger. My "new" ride was parked a few dozen feet in front of them. Having been in the business, I immediately recognized it as anything but new.

At the curb was a 1974-ish Chevrolet 1-ton pickup with an old Holmes 440 series mechanical tow body mounted on it. A massive, amber-tinted acrylic light bar was bolted to the roof. The front bumper hid behind a wide steel plate covered with old tire tread. Two large rubber slings dangled below a rusty iron hook. The forty-year-old truck looked pretty good. A fresh coat of black paint covered much of its age; Jimmy's "Custom & Classic Hauling" logo stenciled on the door broadcast to the world its owner.

They guffawed even after the shock faded from my face. I

ignored my new old truck and walked to Stanley's SUV.

"Haha," I said to the jokesters. "I'm sure it took you weeks to find a truck like my old rig."

"My old rig" meaning the tow truck I briefly drove for my uncle's towing company. The old rig was also the inspiration for the "Hook" nickname my jackass uncle gave me. Except for the color, it was an almost exact duplicate of this truck.

Stick roared with laughter. "It is yer old rig, ya hose head."

Stanley leaned further out the window. "Your uncle says hello," he said with a chuckle. Then he tossed at me a pair of keys joined by a length of twisted copper wire. "Get over to the building on Main. As of now you're back on the hook."

They sped away, their laughter spilling out of the still open windows.

Chapter Thirteen

Common sense told me to go back to bed. Unfortunately, common sense and I aren't on the best of terms so I ignored the suggestion.

I trudged up to the truck – my truck – quite unenthusiastic about my reunion with the old beast. Stick's guys may have put a fresh coat of paint on the outside but through the cracked windshield, I could tell the inside was just as craptastic as the last time I drove it.

Old paperwork littered the dash. Wires for the lights on the roof dangled through the sagging headliner. Dark tan foam peeked through large cracks in the blue vinyl seat covering.

I sighed then grabbed the door handle, jamming my thumb into the black button beneath it just as I'd done hundreds of times in the past. My thumbnail doubled over when the button refused to move.

"Dammit!".

The button didn't budge because the door was locked. Whoever parked it must have associated some delusional sense of value to the truck and vastly overestimated the work ethic of the local car thieves who might brave the subfreezing temperature at the ass-crack of dawn to pull off a low value heist.

Or maybe it was just habit. Either way, I was annoyed that some overcautious prick caused me to spend more time freezing boogers. I rammed the door key into the lock and gave it a violent twist. The mechanism turned stiffly, ending with a dull THUNK and a sharp SNAP. The THUNK was the door unlocking. The SNAP was the old key breaking off in the cylinder.

"Son of a bitch!"

The Jimmy Phone jangled in my pocket. I answered it.

"Use the passenger door, ay," Stick's nasally voice said, "the other one don't work so good."

"No shit, ya snot stuffed Canuck."

I thought that pretty loudly but didn't feel ballsy enough to say it. Instead, I mumbled, "Yeah, I got it" and hung up.

I opened the door and was nearly knocked to my knees by the stench of stale cigarette smoke and rotting mouse carcass. The ashtray dangled open from the bottom of the dash, overflowing with cigarette butts. Jimmy probably wasn't aware that he didn't just buy my uncle's oldest piece of shit tow truck, he also got his bad weather smoking shelter.

I swept a pile of crushed Morley's Non-filtered soft packs and crumpled Burger King bags from the bench seat onto the floor. Grabbing the hard-plastic steering wheel, I pulled myself into the cab. The frozen vinyl seat crackled when I dropped onto it. I heard a muted squeak then felt something sharp pierce my left butt cheek. I bounced my head off the roof and banged my right knee into the gearshift scrambling away from whatever brazen little fucker bit me.

80

I expected to see the gnashing mouth of a hungry mouse or maybe even a small rat peeking out of the cracked vinyl but instead found a broken seat cushion spring jutting through the crumbling foam. Relieved that a case of winter rabies wasn't in my near future, I looked around to make sure no one witnessed my spastic retreat. The street and sidewalks were still empty. Fortunately, I didn't see the gossip twins peering through their windows, either.

I smoothed out a few empty fast-food sacks from the floor and covered my latest pain in the ass with them. I gingerly settled onto the Burger King seat cover and grabbed the wheel. The ignition worked much better than the door lock; it turned easily without the key snapping in half.

The twin exhaust pipes below the rear bumper spewed clouds of black smoke like old tires burning in a coal mine. The sound dampening insulation in the mufflers burned out decades ago, leaving them mufflers in name only. The beast's roar was impressive but unfortunately merely implied considerably more power lurked under the hood than the long-abused engine still possessed.

I ground the gearshift into 1st and lurched onto the street. More oily smoke belched from the rear of the truck. Despite the new paint job, the old rig obviously hadn't seen much maintenance in years.

I shifted gears when the truck began to shake. The rest of the gears ground just as hard as the first. The gauges on the dash fluttered around like hummingbirds on meth. At a moment when they all stabilized I was pleased to see Stick had at least topped off the oil and fuel.

I aimed the old truck toward Main Street, fighting the frosty pavement the whole way. Even though the truck has full-time four-wheel drive, the tires hadn't been replaced since 1986 – what little tread they had was only marginally better than if zig-zaggy lines were drawn on the old rubber with a medium point Sharpie.

Work trucks lined the street in front of the old building. Despite the early hour, a handful of workers in insulated overalls futzed around the fencing while several suits milled about the sidewalk.

I wedged my truck between two local news vans along the curb near the construction site gate. I tromped onto the parking brake to hold the truck in place. I glanced at the shattered side mirror; the unbroken slivers didn't help me much so I looked over my shoulder for oncoming streetcars. It was clear this time.

I kicked open the door. Stanley and Nik were in my face before my boots hit the street.

"About time," he grumped.

"Da," Nik agreed.

Stanley was decked out in a grey wool trench coat; a collared shirt and tie peeked out beneath it. He looked more businessman-ish than former-football-star-ish for a change. Nik had traded his usual garish plaid and polyester for a light grey security guard uniform. A blocky Tazer gun rode high on his right hip. I'd never seen him dressed as a guard before and started to ask about it but his sterner than usual glare paralyzed my tongue.

"Uh, right," was all I got out.

The construction gate was open. A small hydraulic crane swung its boom over the building and stopped. Four workmen carried away a section of fence that blocked the front door of the building. At the side of the building a couple of workers in white, insulated overalls loaded aluminum cases into a moving van. The Amazonian guard stood near a side door watching everyone with a critical eye. The site was really hopping for an early morning during a holiday week.

"Big plans for today?" I asked nonchalantly.

Another worker carried a faux wood podium to the sidewalk and placed it in the new break in the fence. The newsies poured out of their vans and started setting up tripods and cameras at the curb.

"No," Stanley said pointedly. Then he gestured to an old, white Ford Econoline van parked inside the construction area just a few feet beyond the fence. "Tow that truck outta here. It puked its engine and we can't find Dan,"

Large, faded lettering on the side of the van said "JOE" and proclaimed he provides "professional" and "quality" plumbing service; the bashed in fender and missing hubcaps suggested otherwise.

"Dan who?" I asked.

"Dan, the owner of the van," Stanley snapped.

"You mean Joe," I corrected.

"No," Stanley said very quietly, "I mean Dan. Joe's been holding up dirt for years." He scowled. "Who gives a shit who owns it? Quit arguing with me and hook the van. You got fifteen minutes to get it out of here."

Ah, the nearly impossible deadline. How I'd missed those.

"Of course I do," I said rolling my eyes.

"Da," said Nik. "Streetcar starts then."

"Oh, yeah," I conceded.

Nik turned and marched toward a news van parked in front of the gate. He gestured emphatically and issued a few barely intelligible commands until the cameraman skulked into his van and pulled ahead a few feet.

I sighed and hopped back into the truck. Seconds later I was inside the fence and inches away from the van's front bumper. After stomping on the parking brake and shifting the transmission's transfer case into neutral, I left the engine running and climbed out of the truck.

Although it had been years since I last drove the antique wrecker, I still remembered how to operate the balky controls. I tugged a battered lever and watched highly oxidized wire rope unspool from a large reel mounted behind the truck cab. The tow hook inched lazily from the boom onto the frozen mud in front of the van. I looked up and sighed as the crane's heavy iron hook descended 50 feet in mere seconds.

My fingers quickly turned into frozen sausages. Gloves would have been a good idea. I alternated one hand on the lever and one in my coat pocket - that helped frostbite them both equally. The truck engine burbled, occasionally threatening to sputter to a stop, while the cable coiled slowly onto the ground. After several feet unspooled, I let go of the lever and puffed a few blasts of humid air into my cupped hands to warm them.

84

It was temporary relief I regretted pretty quickly. The moisture on my fingertips froze to the tow chains I grabbed from the truck bed. Of course I didn't notice that until tossing the chains under the van with my fingertip skin still stuck to the metal.

"Son of a-"

My hand recoiled in pain, smacking a lurking Stanley in the chest. I jumped in surprise. He didn't flinch.

"Dammit, Stanley, what the hell?" I wheezed.

He tapped the black smartwatch on his wrist.

"Quit screwing around – you're in the way," he said then stepped back a few steps and folded his arms. I'd never admit it to him but his glare was quite motivational.

I scooched under the old van. The noxious fumes from my truck's exhaust hovered near the ground like a petroleum fart. Stanley's feet were a couple yards from my head, one of them tapping impatiently.

I fumbled with the icy chains, struggling to wrap them around the van's frame. The steel was frigid and my hands were numb and uncooperative. The more I hurried the less progress I made.

I paused and shoved my hands into my coat pockets to get a little feeling back into them. A pair of expensive black loafers lurking below dark wool dress pants walked along the van and stopped next to Stanley. Jimmy's voice mixed with the racket of the engine.

I figured Stanley would soon chew my ass for not being done so I got back to work. Sweat soaked my sweatshirt while I fought the uncooperative chains. My truck coughed as I finished. The carburetor dumped in more gas, the engine idled faster and more noisily in response. The buzz of Jimmy and Stanley's conversation increased in volume. The engine quickly adjusted itself again, returning to a low roar – but they didn't seem to notice.

"...and I don't like rushing things," said Stanley.

"We're not discussing this again. We've got to move before we have any more break-ins," Jimmy replied.

Curiosity bested my better judgement. Admittedly, it wasn't much of a tussle. I slid a little closer to the shoes.

"You sure they will buy it?" Stanley asked.

"We'll know soon enough. Let's get the show started," answered Jimmy.

"Ok. I'll get Nik moving."

"Is Butch here yet?"

Before Stanley answered, the engine hesitated then backfired a heavy cloud of oily smoke under the van. I coughed uncontrollably.

The toes of all four dress shoes pointed themselves at my head.

"Hook, you still under there?" Stanley barked.

"*Cough...cough...*yeah...*cough,*" I answered.

"Hurry the fuck up. Get that thing over to the impound lot."

I nearly choked. I rolled out from underneath the van and looked up at them.

"The impound lot?" I croaked. "You didn't say anything about the impound lot."

Stanley grinned and shoved some papers into my coat pocket. Jimmy shrugged. Then they walked away in opposite directions,

Stanley going to the rear of the building, Jimmy out to the street. I shivered but not because of the weather.

Chapter Fourteen

You see, the reason why my ex, Samantha, was such a ginormously huge mistake was because her dad is a cop. One reason of many, really. Oh, and her pop wasn't just any cop: I was assigned to his shift when I was a trainee.

I swear I didn't even know Lieutenant Assante, the crotchety old fuck, even had a daughter. When I met the leggy, blue-eyed redhead, her family tree was the furthest thing from my mind; my interest was only in her limbs. She conveniently neglected to mention her familial ties until I was handcuffed into a relationship with her. Literally. She whispered it off-handedly while she had me naked and handcuffed to a chair.

It was pretty well known on the force that Samantha's lazy old Lieutenant daddy couldn't spot a crook in a prison yard during exercise hour. Yet somehow he figured out I was her new boyfriend.

The grouchy prick didn't like me much when he met me as a trainee. Hell, he didn't really like anyone who wasn't a 30-year veteran. But he really hated me when he learned I was with Sam. I was fired in short order – but not for dating his little angel, no, that wasn't good enough. Instead, I was let go for "leaking details of ongoing cases."

I told him and anyone who would listen I never tipped off any suspects but it didn't matter. Regardless, someone really was passing on information about investigations and he was furious that Sam and I were basically living together; I was a convenient scapegoat to solve two of his nagging problems.

It takes a very special woman to stay with an unemployed man. Turned out Samantha wasn't all that special. Even though I picked up the towing job at my uncle's company, she dropped me like a hot, minimum wage rock. Despite the breakup, Lieutenant Assante still hated my guts and made it one of the missions in his life to make my life miserable.

His hate for me intensified when Jimmy suggested – correctly – to Sgt. Stevens that the mole in the department was actually Samantha. As lazy and inept as he was, the Lieutenant couldn't be bought and was very proud of that fact. That no one ever felt the need to buy him off because he was lazy and inept was inconsequential. Samantha had been selling bits of information she'd heard from him at the family supper table. Her arrest deeply embarrassed him but that wasn't nearly as big of a blow to his veteran cop ego as was his reassignment from his shift command. Reassigned to babysitting the...

"HOOK!" Stanley snapped. "I said get that to the impound lot. NOW!"

...reassigned to babysitting the department's impound lot.

"Yessir," I mumbled.

I grabbed the winch controls and retracted the cable. The bare chains scraped noisily across the van's bumper as its front tires rose slowly off the ground. Most car owners hate that cosmetic damage but I wasn't in a very caring mood. My thoughts were focused on the impound lot, hoping that my old L-T was on holiday vacation. A metallic groan from inside the van jerked me back to reality. I let go of the lever and went back to the van to check it out.

All its doors were locked. I peered through the frosty windshield. I didn't see anything broken, just the usual array of pipes, hoses, fittings, and a padded mover's blanket covering a large toolbox or water heater. I shrugged it off and went back to the controls.

The engine on the crane revved. I paused to watch. The operator, hunched over the controls, simultaneously raised and extended its boom while retracting the cable. The old safe from the basement, dangling from a sling, slowly rose from the rear of the building. It looked rustier than I remembered and the script seemed less shiny. Of course, it was 50 feet in the air in the chilly morning's pale gray overcast light. I figured the obnoxious halogen work lamps in the basement cast it in, well a different light.

A matte black armored truck with "Secure Express" in silver block lettering on the doors rolled up to the gate. It parked where the news van had been. My jaw dropped at the sight of the common immigrant cab driver, Nik, behind its steering wheel.

Nik jumped down from the cab and walked over to me. I stepped toward him but was stopped abruptly by a massive hand on my shoulder.

"Hook, would you get the hell out of here?" Stanley growled.

I had questions – many questions – but my finely honed observational skills told me to keep them to myself. Nik strode past me and stopped at the incapacitated van. He removed a key from a clip on his belt, unlocked the driver's side door, and leaned inside. He fiddled with its controls for a moment then got back out and relocked it. He strode over to me with a severe look on his face.

"Eez in neutral. You go now," he said, shooshing me away with his gloved hands.

"Uh, sure," I said to his back as he trudged back to the sidewalk by his armored truck.

I opened my rig's door and carefully eased my ass onto the fast food bags. I swung my legs into the cab. The broken door key dangling below the steering column snagged my jeans, tearing a hole in my pants and ripping the ignition key out of the cylinder.

The key ring mocked me from the pile of garbage on the floorboards while the engine still rumbled. I reached to the ignition and turned it. Even without a key, it spun. The engine sputtered to a stop. Out of the corner of my eye I saw a glowering Stanley move toward me. I clutched and twisted the ignition the other direction. Sans key, the engine still labored back to life.

I looked at Stanley. He walked back to the crane without noticing I'd upgraded the old tow truck to keyless entry and keyless ignition. I shrugged and put my truck into gear and rolled forward a few feet.

The blast of a train whistle caused me to jam on the brakes. A street car zipped past the grill of my truck. I didn't turn but in my peripheral vision I saw Nik shake his head and walk away. After the last cabin of the streetcar whizzed by I pulled onto Main and headed north toward the impound lot.

JEFF DEITERING

Chapter Fifteen

The KCPD Vehicle Impound Lot is in the northeast part of Kansas City, nestled against the south bank of the Missouri River. Officers on double secret, unofficial probation get assigned to this crappy location. The facility itself isn't that bad, but the Glen J. Hopkins memorial sewage treatment plant a few hundred feet to the west is often very...odiferous. Unfortunately for the poor saps working at the lot, the wind is almost always from the west.

The ten-minute drive to the lot allowed my old tow truck to finally warm up a bit. The engine smoothed noticeably, only misfiring every mile instead of two or three times a block. Even the air trickling from the dashboard vents changed from icy to nearly tepid.

The thought of seeing my ex's jackass father was bad. The reality was actually worse. As I neared the impound lot office I saw that Lt. Assante was indeed working. He was in a heated discussion with some schmuck in the parking lot. Unfortunately, also in the lot was his longtime toady, Detective Holstein.

Sgt. Holstein, I mean – he lost his detective title for not detecting his best friend's daughter as a mole. A tall, round, lump of inept laziness, he rarely speaks and when he does, it's usually in very short words that don't always go together. After his reassignment to patrol duty it was no secret that most of his shift was spent patrolling the impound office break room with his buddy Assante.

Most cops are outstanding, selfless public servants. But, like any other job, KCPD has a couple of lackluster employees that embarrass the rest of the force: Assante and Holstein. Individually they're colossal dickheads. Together they're the bad cop-worse cop duo known to both crooks and fellow cops as Ass-Hole.

Holstein leaned against a slush-covered squad car, his right hand resting on the PR-24 baton dangling from his belt. He favored speaking with the club when he ran out of little words to grunt.

The vaguely-familiar looking schmuck swayed unsteadily as Assante, bent forward at the waist, stared directly into the guy's Adam's apple and jabbed an accusatory finger into the poor bastard's baggy Sporting KC soccer team jersey. Napoleon would have heartily approved of the officer's style. It was a classic Ass-Hole ploy where Assante verbally instigated a conflict while Holstein waited to intervene with his baton.

The pasty slacker's dirty blond dreadlocks spilling from under a multicolored rastacap flapped in the breeze – the breeze or Assante's shouting. He wavered slightly but otherwise seemed unfazed by either Assante or the freezing weather. RayBan Wayfarers obscured eyes that I assumed were as bloodshot as his slouch was indifferent. The dude was obviously baked which appeared to further aggravate Assante.

I put my head down and drove past the parking lot shout-fest.

I stopped in front of the impound area gate and took a quick look at Stanley's paperwork. Smiling, I trotted inside the small administrative office building. I hoped to complete the in-take process before Ass-Hole finished berating the stoner.

I knew the cop behind the counter, Officer Engstrom, a rookie recently trained by Sgt. Stevens. About 2 inches taller than Assante but without the girth of thirty years of donuts, she's generally a good cop. She had to have pissed off a higher-up pretty bad to get stuck with clerk duty for Assante. That actually wasn't a surprise to me. I hoped she forgotten our previous misunderstandings: she'd tried to arrest me twice and nearly shot me one other time.

This time, however, she wasn't interested in me. Her eyes were glued to a small television perched on the corner of her desk. Her police radio crackled with nonstop traffic. Getting Dan's or Joe's or whoever-the-hell's crummy old plumbing van entered into the system quickly looked unlikely.

"Um, excuse me. I, uh, have a van to dump off here and-"

"Shut it!" she commanded without breaking her gaze from the TV.

I shifted impatiently from foot to foot. My hope for a speedy exit withered. I looked through a window behind me; the rasta-slacker stood alone, peering through the impound area's 12-foot tall chain-link fence.

The Lieutenant and his lackey popped through a side door.

"...like I was going to release a car to that hophead, Did ya get a whiff of him? He stunk more than the shit plant," Assante was saying.

Holstein responded with his own expert opinion.

"Uh huh."

Assante turned and saw me. His jocularity evaporated instantly, replaced with an irate squint.

"What the hell are you doing-"

"L-T," Engstrom interrupted, pointing to the television, "you should see this."

"Quiet, Rookie!"

"Uh, sir," she replied, "you really need to watch this."

The chatter and bursts of static on the police radio increased. Assante straightened at the "sir," pausing at the rare show of respect. He strutted around the counter like a 3-star general and stood behind Engstrom to watch her TV. She bristled at the condescending chauvinist resting a hand on her chair back but he didn't notice.

Curiosity trumped my disdain for the old fart; I stepped to the side of the counter to get a view of the screen. Holstein, not wanting to be left out, lumbered over to watch as well.

The small screen was filled with shaky video of what looked like several HotWheels cars zigzagging around model buildings. However, the crawl at the bottom of the screen announced I was seeing live "BREAKING NEWS" brought to me by NewsChopper 3.

I looked more closely. It was in fact an armored truck – Nik's armored truck – leading two very real black Escalades, one with a heavily damaged driver's side door – through the brick building lined grid of streets in central Kansas City. Three navy blue police cars hugged the SUV's tails, their garish red and blue rollers lighting up the frosty streets like trailer park Christmas displays.

The crawl continued with "Secret Room Discovered...Historic safe being delivered to UMKC." I thought it was a bit dramatic for Jimmy to orchestrate a police escort for his crew when the University of Missouri's Kansas City campus was only a few miles from the downtown construction site.

"So, Jimmy's guys are moving an old safe. Big deal," I scoffed.

One of the SUVs sped up and rammed the ass end of the armored truck. My razor sharp deductive abilities slogged into motion. I realized what looked like Jimmy's crew really wasn't.

Engstrom glared at me.

"The SUVs started hassling the armored truck a couple minutes ago," she said.

Nik took a hard left onto 27th Street, the heavy truck cornering as though the street was covered with superglue. The four-wheel drive SUV drivers weren't quite as aggressive and slowed perceptibly, giving Nik some separation. The police cruisers raced up to the SUVs.

Having first-hand knowledge of the street conditions, I mentioned "They should take it easy – the streets are a little slick yet."

"We," Assante said as though he was still a street cop, "are trained for these conditions."

The helicopter's camera panned to the cruisers. The lead squad car found a patch of glare ice and fishtailed wildly. It ricocheted off the left curb over to the right gutter before shimmying back under control. One of its tin hubcaps popped loose and bounced off a light pole.

"See?" Holstein asked smugly.

A trailing cruiser hit another ice patch. Its trunk slowly rotated past its hood. The news chopper focused onto the skidding squad car. It bounced onto the sidewalk and slammed trunk-first into a pawnshop's brick storefront. The camera pulled back out and panned away as two angry officers beat their fists on the roof of the car.

"Yep," I replied, eliciting scowls from all three officers.

Nik and the Escalades turned onto Troost Avenue, a main downtown thoroughfare. The two remaining squad cars slowed and fell further behind.

"Seems like a lot of fuss over a safe full of that Black Hand stuff," I said.

Assante shook his head.

"Pffft. There's nothing about the Black Hand in there; that's an urban legend, dumbass. It's got lists of all the cops and politicians who were ever on the take. Hundreds of names. Prominent names. That's what's in the safe," he said then returned his attention to the screen.

Newschopper 3 focused on the truck as it neared a large intersection with 39th Street. The signal was red and a few unlucky saps out and about during the post-Christmas dead time plodded across Nik's path. Rather than slow down, though, the armored truck unexpectedly surged, accelerating toward the lazy traffic.

The SUVs, probably sensing an accident would stop their prey for them, slowed. Nik locked the brakes on the massive truck, initiating a skid. After a quarter turn, the back tires started spinning, spraying the sidewalks and traffic with sand the city crews had coated the streets for traction. For the second time in as many mornings – on slick surfaces, no less – Nik executed a perfect Rockford turn. He spun the truck 180 degrees, pointing back at the pursuing Escalades.

The rear wheels hopped several times as the truck finished its sudden change of direction then lurched toward the oncoming SUVs. Both Escalades skidded with their antilock brakes struggling to preserve control as Nik aimed his armored battering ram at them.

One of the SUVs slid in front the other. An instant later Nik bashed his truck into the side of the lead SUV. The force of the collision knocked the front Escalade into the trailing one, spinning both away from the unscathed armored truck. Gray steam billowed from the second SUV's grill.

The armored truck stopped in the middle of the street, poised to ram the SUVs again. The Escalade drivers must have sensed nothing good was in their immediate future: they zipped around Nik and split at the intersection, one heading east, the other west. The police cruisers slowly approached the accident scene. The officers wisely decided to stop to assist the undamaged armored truck rather than further embarrass themselves by continuing their unsuccessful "high-speed" chase.

None of us could believe what the hell we just saw. Rasta-man broke the silence by walking inside. We all turned to him.

"Dude, so you got my cab yet?"

"Oh, sure, I got yer cab. The valet will bring it around front for you. Now, get the hell out of here," Assante snorted.

The hophead looked at a crumpled piece of paper in his hands then at Assante for a moment.

"Cool," he said, then shuffled silently back outdoors.

"And quit parking on snow routes!" Assante shouted after him. He and Holstein guffawed.

"20 degrees out there and that shitheel's dressed like it's summer!" Assante said.

"Ha, ha, summer," Holstein parroted.

"Yeah, what an asshole," I chimed in with a chuckle.

The laughter stopped abruptly. My hindsight being nearly 20-20, I probably shouldn't have pushed it using "asshole" with Ass-Hole in the room but I couldn't help myself.

"Why the hell are you even here?"

I dropped onto the counter the papers Stanley gave me.

"Dropoff," I said, gesturing with my thumb over my shoulder toward my truck parked outside the storefront style entrance.

"We aren't Penders' private parking lot. Get that piece of shit," Assante snorted, then corrected himself, "both those pieces of shit – out of here."

Lard-butt Holstein snickered. Even by-the-books Engstrom smirked.

He obviously didn't read the forms Stanley had given me. Fortunately, I had.

"Mr. Penders has nothing to do with it; that order to impound is from Sgt. Stevens," I said very innocently. Then, without letting my brain have any say, my mouth blurted "You know him, right? He arrested your daughter not too long ago."

Assante turned crimson. Holstein's jaw slackened even more than usual. Engstrom looked down, struggling to suppress a smile.

The angry Lieutenant clenched his jaw and practically leapt over the counter to face me. He jabbed a finger into my chest just like he'd done with the stoner. From the corner of my eye I saw Holstein move his right hand to his baton.

"Get the hell out of my office!" he shouted.

"Uh, Hook?" Engstrom said.

"Little busy here, Engstrom," I said, looking down into the beady eyes of Lieutenant Half-pint.

"I'm not leaving until the van is off my hook," I said.

He grabbed the tow order from the counter and tore it in half, dropping the pieces at my feet.

"Fine," I said with a sigh. "You can explain to Stevens why you refused an impound order. Oh, and tell Samantha she still owes me a TV and a couch," I finished with a very insincere grin.

"Go fuck yourself," he said dismissively.

"Hey, you ungrateful little prick, she's lucky I didn't press charges," I popped off without thinking.

Engstrom tried again to insert herself into our spat.

"Lieutenant?"

"Not now, Rookie!" he said, waving her off. He turned his gaze back to me, this time with an insincere smile of his own.

"Are you really that fucking stupid? I started taking her to the range when she was six years old – she could shoot the nuts off a mosquito by the time she was 10," he said, jabbing me in the chest again. "You're lucky she wasn't serious."

My mouth dropped open. She told me she'd never fired a gun in her life. My lips struggled to release a scathing retort but nothing came out. Thankfully, Officer Engstrom interrupted us one more time, before I sputtered and embarrassingly weak "oh, yeah?"

"Will you two SHUT UP?" she practically shouted. "That loser is stealing your truck!"

All four of us looked out the windows as the slacker jerkily completed a U-turn with my tow truck and chugged away from the office.

Aw, shit.

Chapter Sixteen

The slacker slouched in the seat of my truck and cruised past the office. He looked at me through the door, gave a lazy wave, and sputtered away. The convenience of keyless entry suddenly didn't seem so convenient.

I looked expectantly at the three cops.

Considering who was in the room I knew it was wasted breath but I had to ask. "Well, aren't you going to do something?"

Assante and Holstein looked at each other and burst into laughter. Engstrom stared at her feet.

"I figured as much," I said, heading for the door.

I didn't know what I'd do once I was outside but it didn't matter. Instead of seeing the flickering taillights of my truck I was greeted with the oncoming running lights of a black Cadillac Escalade. It rolled to a stop in front of me.

Jimmy exited from the driver's door and walked around to me. Considering his "mystery of history" was almost stolen just minutes earlier, he looked remarkably calm.

"Lose something, Hook?" he asked as my tow truck rumbled to a stop behind the SUV. The engine wheezed for several seconds before dying with a final backfire.

Stanley and the stoner exited my truck and walked over to us. All three looked expectantly at me.

I shifted my weight from foot to foot, hoping someone would speak. Jimmy's eyes bored into me without blinking. The stoner swayed unsteadily in the frigid breeze. Stanley merely scowled like he usually did. A few dried tree leaves rattled across the driveway pavement.

"What?" I finally asked.

Jimmy answered.

"I asked you to tow the van here. Instead, we find Terry leaving here with your truck – and the van," he said shaking his head in disappointment.

"I tried to drop the van but that ass-wipe Assante wouldn't take it. Then this strung-out tool swiped my truck when they didn't give him back his car."

The stoner pointed at me and started to speak but Stanley cut him off.

"We don't have time for this bullshit," he said then strode to the office entrance. Jimmy and the stoner followed. Sensing an entertaining confrontation, I shrugged to no one in particular and went inside to watch too.

Stanley picked up the torn impound orders from the floor. He slapped them down on the counter and straightened to his full 6'-5" height directly in front of Assante.

The lieutenant glared at everyone in his office, focusing on

Jimmy last. He tilted his head from side-to-side, cracking the joints in his neck, then straightened again, puffing out his chest.

"You don't run this place, *I* do," he huffed.

Everyone stared expectantly at him as the gears under his hat churned. He'd tried for years to find an excuse to arrest Jimmy, convinced that my enigmatic boss was some elusive underworld mastermind. Hell, even I wasn't sure that he wasn't but I knew it would take a better cop than Assante to figure that out.

Instead of more bluster, Assante glanced at his watch then reached to his clip-on tie and pretended to straighten it. Turning to Engstrom, he said, "Fuck this, I'm on break. Rookie, take care of them," then left through a back hallway. Holstein looked around the room, stuffed his hands into his pockets, and then shuffled down the hall after Assante.

Stanley didn't give them a chance to return.

"Kristine," he said to Officer Engstrom, "Can you help Terry with his cab?" he asked with a politeness I rarely witnessed firsthand.

Maybe she was influenced by his charm but I doubted it. More likely she saw an opportunity to annoy Assante merely by helping us.

"Sure," she said, rolling her chair back to her computer screen.

I finally remembered "Terry" as the baked asshole who refused to give me a ride when I was being chased by Cuban kidnappers but that's a long story for another time. Stanley, however, seemed inexplicably chummy with him.

I turned to Jimmy. "Who the hell is Terry?"

"He's one of Nik's drivers," he said with zero elaboration.

I didn't know Nik had "drivers." I couldn't fathom Nik hiring someone like Terry either, but again, Nik is a unique common immigrant so I swallowed my curiosity.

Terry pulled a handful of papers from his front pocket and placed them on the counter. He carefully separated a few ZigZags from a larger sheet and stuffed those back into his pocket. He smoothed the wrinkled document with a few swipes of his hand and pushed it across the counter to Officer Engstrom.

Engstrom glanced at it, tapped a few keys on her computer keyboard, and then left the building. A minute later she returned in a grungy red taxi, parking it near the entrance. Terry bumped fists with Stanley then walked to the door.

He paused and turned to Stanley, Jimmy, and me.

"Dudes," he said, then nodded to Engstrom and added, "Dude-ette."

He flashed us a "V" sign with his hand.

"Peace," he said with a loopy grin then got in his cab and drove away.

I figured Terry's predicament was way more of a hassle than my simple drop-off. I was encouraged: without Assante in the room, it went pretty smoothly.

"Hey," I said to Stanley and Jimmy, "The Ass-Holes are still on break; I got this now."

They glanced at each other, silently deciding who would speak. Jimmy nodded and crossed his arms.

"With all the excitement already this morning, I think we'll hang around to make sure this gets done right," Stanley said.

I noticed Engstrom was smirking again and not even trying to hide it from me. I sighed and slid the torn orders over to her.

Assante's voice drifted in from the breakroom down the hall.

"Are they outa here yet?"

Engstrom turned to the hallway and shouted back to him "just about!"

"Grouchy fucker," I said.

"It's a lot worse now," she replied, rolling her eyes.

I tilted my head, raising my eyebrows in question.

She leaned toward me conspiratorially. "His daughter missed her hearing last week and skipped out on the bail he put up."

She looked side to side to make sure no one overheard. Satisfied I was the only recipient of her gossip, she moved back to her keyboard. She entered my information then reached under the countertop.

"Gate's open," she said. "Drop it in space G-13."

I got back into my truck. I crinkled my nose at the contact odor of Terry that hung faintly in the cold air; I rolled down my window about half-way when the mechanism seized up.

"Dammit," I griped while driving through the automatic gate Officer Engstrom had opened for me.

I'd gotten to know the impound lot pretty well in the couple of years I spent with my uncle's towing company so I easily found slot G-13. I disconnected the old van and was back at the gate within a couple of minutes.

As the gate reopened for me to exit, I saw Jimmy and Stanley get into their Escalade and drive away. I drove off the lot, waving to Engstrom through the security camera aimed at the gate. I'm sure she appreciated the friendly gesture.

Chapter Seventeen

Stanley didn't give me any new orders so I drove back toward my loft, first stopping at Dea's coffee shop, *Brew Tea and the Beanst*.

The *Beanst* used to be a local stop 'n' rob gas station stocked with generic soda pop, stale junk food, beer by the can, and lottery tickets. I dined there often.

Dea bought the old inconvenience store and updated it with an 18th century French motif. Out went the old metal shelves, noisy beer coolers, and rolling wiener warmer. In came fresh pastries, exotic teas, flavored coffees, and gift cards. If not for the bajillion calorie cinnamon rolls I would never step foot in the hipster filled place. Well, if not for cinnamon rolls and Dea, of course.

The original checkout counter was replaced with a glass pastry case, the cigarette display case discarded for a large chalkboard menu listing in a flowery font the *Beanst* menu of beverages and baked goods. Images of large wild boars in velvet suits and delicate roses covered the formerly smoke-stained walls. The aroma from Dea's oven and coffee roaster was a welcomed improvement over the stagnant gas station air.

I couldn't bring myself to mingle with the millennial dip-wads mooching free Wi-Fi from the booths in the seating area. Instead, I walked to the pastry display case. I leaned against the counter near the cash register and waited while Dea cleared a table vacated by a self-absorbed twenty-something in skinny jeans, Lennon glasses, and a trilby hat.

Dea's ponytail bounced as she returned to the front of the shop. Even in a shapeless polyester brown frock, she still made my heart thump a little funny. I grinned at her like a goofy puppy getting a new Frisbee.

"Good morning?" she asked.

"It's getting better," I replied, raising my eyebrows suggestively.

I reached across the counter to touch her hand. The cuff of my coat bumped a Mason jar full of pens next to the register. It fell over and scattered half-empty ballpoints all over the countertop.

Dea shook her head as I scrambled to round up the pens. After I'd corralled all the Bics back into the jar she grabbed my hand, possibly out of affection but more likely to prevent me from knocking over anything else.

"Um, yeah, it was kind of a, uh, crazy day," I said. "Stanley had me move an old van before the press conference started. I ran into Ass and Hole at the impound lot. Well, not physically ran into them, just had to talk to the motherfu- er, uh, jerks. I even watched one of the weirdest car chases I've ever seen. It was like watching a bunch of toys. And the cops, man, those guys were..."

Her eye roll at me stopped my jabbering narrative.

"So, yeah: crazy day," I finished quietly.

She smiled halfheartedly. She knew working for Jimmy Penders was generally crazy damn near every day – generally in different ways – but crazy none the less.

"I watched the press conference. And the chase. Jimmy better have some extra guards at the university – this is too big for the school's student security officers to handle," she said.

"Psh, of course he has," I replied, hoping she didn't realize it never occurred to me that someone would try for the safe again. I was beginning to wonder if maybe Dea wouldn't be a more useful employee for Jimmy than I was.

"I can't wait to see what they find inside it," she said, her eyes glazing over like they always did when her mind drifted back to the rampant violence and corruption of Kansas City's Roaring 20s. I gave her hand a gentle squeeze to bring her back to the present. She snapped into focus and looked at my grease-smudged hand.

"Oh, yeah, I'm towing for Jimmy again," I explained.

"I know – Stanley told me last week. *Back on the hook* is how he phrased it, laughing like it was the funniest thing ever."

I winced.

"You talked to Stanley?"

"Sure. We talk all the time. He lets me review his lecture notes," she replied.

"He's taking a class?" I asked incredulously.

"Don't be silly," she replied with a chuckle. "He teaches a contemporary business practices class at UMKC."

So, Stanley was a professor – something he told my girlfriend but never mentioned to me. A twinge of jealousy surged through me. I'd practically saved his life but all that got me was he didn't threaten to rip out my spine quite so often. Then I remembered I'd lost over $100,000 worth of company SUVs in less than a day and decided maybe he had cause for keeping me at arm's length.

"You want to stop up later?" I asked, wiggling my eyebrows as lecherously as I could.

"Sure."

That made me smile.

The Jimmy Phone buzzed in my pocket.

That made me frown.

"Dammit. Just a sec," I said fumbling for the phone while moving a few steps away from the counter to take the call. I didn't expect to get yelled at but somehow most of my calls end up pretty loud and I didn't need Dea or her customers hearing anything.

"Go for Hook," I said, winking at my girlfriend.

"Don't be a tool," Stanley said loud enough for Dea to hear. She giggled as I took a few more steps away from her.

"Sorry," I mumbled.

"Whatever. Meet Jimmy and me at the KC Ice Center at 5:30."

"Right, 5:30. Wait – where did you say?"

"KC Ice Center. On Johnson Drive."

I already knew where it was, it just seemed like an odd place to meet. It was an ice skating rink.

Samantha once told me we should go ice skating, so of course

I bought a pair of figure skates and taught myself how to skate. Or at least taught myself not to fall down every few seconds. Of course, Sam was just being her random self and we never did go ice skating.

"Is this a company skating party? I should probably bring my skates – those rentals smell like spoiled gym socks filled with raw sewage," I said.

His exasperated sigh crackled my phone's speaker.

"We're not skating, you moron. Just be there at 5:30."

"Er, sure."

Something Dea said flickered in my dome. I shielded my mouth and phone with my hand.

"Hey, uh, Stan," I said, lowering my voice. "I think it might be a good idea to put some extra guards on the safe, ya know, in case someone tries to bust into it again."

"Don't worry, the safe is safe," he said chuckling as he hung up on me.

I pocketed the phone and returned to Dea still waiting at the register.

"I, uh, gotta go. I need to check on Patch and then go meet Jimmy and Stan."

I gave her a peck on the forehead.

"See you after work," I said with smile.

"You bet," she replied with a smile of her own. "I really miss Patch."

My smile faded.

Chapter Eighteen

Patch was asleep on the kitchen counter when I got back to the loft. Well into what was probably his third 3-hour nap of the day, he merely lowered his left ear to acknowledge I was home.

I draped my coat over the back of a stool near the snoozing feline and shuffled to the bathroom to shower off the frozen sweat and grease. I thawed under the scalding water for several minutes scraping away most of the grime. I splashed on a fresh dose of Old Spice then dressed in another pair of jeans and a red sweatshirt from the fairly-clean pile of clothes on the floor.

Patch had moved his nap to the couch by the time I came back into the main room. I nuked another slice of leftover pizza in the kitchen. The microwave hardened the stale cheese and dehydrated the pineapple bits but the spicy grease from the pepperoni covered those imperfections. I sat next to Patch and ate the pizza off a folded paper towel, using it as a napkin when I finished. I wadded it into a small ball. The muffled crinkling pulled Patch from his nap.

I tossed the paper ball onto the floor. The suddenly alert Patch launched from the couch onto the floor and pounced on it. After batting it around for a few moments, he chomped into his paper prey then shook his fuzzy little head violently. After ensuring the ball was no longer a threat, he trotted back to me and dropped his kill at my feet. I picked it up and tossed it again, starting the hunt anew. We played fetch for fifteen minutes, the game finally ending with a winded Patch lying on top of the tattered paper ball rather than retrieving it.

I snorted at my cat for tiring so easily then dozed off myself. A few hours later Patch jumped onto my lap, startling me awake.

"Wha...hey?"

He reached out with a paw and touched me on the cheek. Then he hopped onto the coffee table and sat beside my cell phones. He flicked his tail, swiping it across my personal phone. The screen came to life letting me know it was nearly 5 o'clock.

"Oh, shit! I gotta run," I blurted. Patch looked at me for a moment then proceeded to clean his privates. I hastily put on my Carhartt coat and stumbled into my boots. I felt guilty for not refreshing his 3-hour old water but I figured he would be ok for another hour or so.

"I'll be back soon," I promised while opening the loft door. Patch paused his bath to blink in response then resumed washing his nethers.

The KC Ice Center is in the suburb of Shawnee nestled in a complex of volleyball courts and softball fields. On a good day on dry pavement with a decent vehicle it was half an hour away. I rolled into the parking lot 40 minutes and one loud Stanley phone call later.

Out of habit, I parked my rig next to the bread-and-butter of the towing industry, an aging Ford pick-up. The air felt slightly warmer though still plenty cold enough to see my breath. I stuffed my hands into my coat pockets and walked across the lot to the skate complex.

The community facility has two rinks: one outdoors under a large steel frame and sheet metal roof, the other a more traditional indoor rink. Stanley didn't say in which part they'd be. I paused inside the concession area between the two rinks. It teemed with kids clomping around the battered carpeting in rented skates and their parents scowling at spending a frigid day inside a slightly less frigid building.

I took a guess that Jimmy and Stanley would seek at least a little comfort and walked to my right to the indoor rink. The humid air was a smidgen warmer than outdoors and thick with the powerful aroma of stale ice, frozen sweat, and crushed professional aspirations.

Young boys and girls awkwardly practiced figure skating while their parents stared at their cell phones and drank Venti Starbucks in the bleachers; Dea would have winced at the sight. I scanned the crowd looking for my boss but didn't see him. I felt the creeped-out glare of a young skating instructor silently telling me she didn't appreciate a lone guy gawking at her students or their parents. I decided to move along to the other rink.

While passing through the concession area, my stomach was lured to the counter by the overpowering aroma of fried food and cheap beer. Stanley already knew I'd be late so I gave in to my gastric urges and stopped to grab a snack.

119

I strolled out to the outdoor rink munching on a polish dog with the works, pausing between a pair of small aluminum grand stands that would look more at home at a middle school soccer pitch than a hockey rink. Two high-hat patio heaters blazed away, warming everything within an 18-inch radius. I moved under one and watched the action on the ice while eating my polish dog.

A half-dozen adults in hockey gear milled around the ice, passing pucks around, some making a racket by practicing slapshots at the sidewalls. A puck suddenly whistled through the air and bounced off the Plexiglas in front of me.

I instinctively – and needlessly – dropped my snack and covered my face with my arm. The skater who'd shot the puck glided past, banging his stick against the glass. I glanced down at the remains of my dog covered in snow-melt crystals. Without thinking, I glared and flipped him the bird. My heart skipped a beat when I realized it was Stick. I hoped the grumpy grease monkey couldn't get through the glass any easier than the puck. He parted his lips baring a white mouthguard that had jagged fangs drawn on it then skated away.

I took a closer look at the other skaters on the ice. The only two I didn't recognize as members of Sticks's garage crew were a very attractive raven-haired woman in goalie gear and an extremely nervous referee who looked barely old enough to drive.

A handful of other men sat scattered throughout the stands, more of Stick's knuckle-dragging wrench-turners. They gazed dispassionately at the ice, sipping beer from small, translucent plastic cups.

I spied Jimmy and Stanley in dark insulated coats standing outside the glass near the far goal. I waved a hand to get their attention.

"Yo, Jimmy! Stanley!" I shouted.

I got the stink-eye from everyone in the stands – but not Jimmy and Stanley. Instead, they turned away, shrinking into their coats.

It occurred to me they were trying not to draw attention to themselves. I stopped waving.

After the spectators returned their attention back to the ice, I walked sheepishly past the grandstands to the end of the rink.

"Um, yeah, I'm here."

"We noticed," Jimmy said, still hunched up inside his coat.

Stanley mumbled "idiot" which unfortunately I still heard over the scrapes of the constantly moving skates.

"Er, right. What's up?" I asked.

Stick smacked the Plexiglas near us with another puck. Even though I saw it coming I still flinched. Jimmy and Stanley didn't move a millimeter.

Showoffs.

Jimmy pointed at Stick who nodded in reply.

Stick looked to the end of the rink where six more guys were gearing up.

"Where the hell you guys been? Yer late. Let's GO!" Stick barked.

The rest of his guys hopped over the wall and lined up to start a game. The beautiful goalie donned a blood red helmet with gold eagle heads painted on both sides of it. She smacked her stick on the ice and slid from side to side of the crease like a caged predator.

The teenager dropped the puck at center ice and hurriedly backed away.

"When did Stick hire a chick?" I asked loud enough to be heard over the game.

Stanley chuckled and shook his head. "That's Dorothy," he replied in an equally elevated volume.

"Er, Ok. So, when did Stick hire a Dorothy?"

Jimmy looked at his shoes and sighed.

"Dorothy, our dispatcher," Jimmy said. My befuddlement was quickly replaced with panic. I'd never met our dispatcher but I knew who she was: she was Nik's wife. I was pretty sure he would dismember me slowly and stuff me in an oil drum if he thought I looked at his wife inappropriately.

"You better hope she didn't hear you call her chick – she doesn't like that," Jimmy added.

The left wing drifted too close to her goal. She lowered a shoulder and jarred him off his skates, sending him sprawling across the ice. The pimply-faced ref brought the whistle to his lips then saw her stony glare from inside her helmet. He dropped the whistle and skated away.

"Uh, yeah."

Stanley's phone buzzed. He glanced at the screen for a moment and frowned.

"We need to pick this up," he said to Jimmy. Then he turned to me and asked, "You still have that fake police uniform?"

I bristled at the question. He meant the uniform I'd worn when I still had my own towing business. I found that painting my truck the same midnight blue color as the KCPD squad cars, calling my company "Service Towing," and wearing dark navy polyester pants and a shirt with an official Dragnet Fan Club badge on the left pocket was a great motivator for people at accident scenes to sign off on my higher than standard towing fees. I was very profitable right up until my last client filed a complaint with the city and got my business license revoked. I had little choice but to go to work for Jimmy after that. I should get rid of it but for practical reasons I kept it.

"Of course I still have it – I use it for my T-1000 costume at Planet Comicon," I answered. Then I added in a deep voice, "Have you seen this boy?"

Stanley's jaw dropped, quivering as though he wanted to say something but nothing came out. I quickly deduced he was not into pop culture cosplay.

"Go home and put it on. Use the belt and holster in here," he said, shoving a small duffel bag into my stomach.

"What? Did you say holster?" I asked, hoping the din of the game caused me to mishear him. It occurred to me that we met at the ice rink so no one could easily eavesdrop on us but since we had to practically shout at one another it seemed somewhat self-defeating.

"Yeah, for your old Glock."

I started to protest but Stanley cut me off. "There's a new front sight for it in the duffel bag. Ammo, too, so be sure to load it."

The last time Stanley asked me to carry, my Glock fell out of my pants onto a sidewalk and broke off the front sight. Then I accidentally killed a parking meter with it.

"Um, Ok. Why?"

"Some of Stevens' officers were guarding the safe but he had to pull them off," Jimmy explained. "Go change then get over to Kokafear Hall at the university. Dr. Benton will meet you there and show you where to stand." He paused then lurched with a sudden thought. "And for god's sake," he added, "don't touch anything."

I looked at Stanley.

"You want me to play security guard again? This is how you have it covered?" I asked sarcastically.

He shrugged.

"Plans change. Besides, it's in your work contract under the Other Duties as Assigned section."

I started reminding him I'd never actually seen my contract but was drowned out by a savage collision into the boards in front of us. The right winger – one of Stick's new autobody men who is brilliant with bondo but dumb as a left-handed pencil – checked Stick into the wall, sliding his face across the glass leaving behind a trail of gooey saliva and boogers. I wanted to smile – I really, really wanted to. But, I knew that Stick was prone to retaliation so I bit my lip.

To confirm my concern, Stick spun around and took a swing at the aggressor. Unhurt by the gloved punch, the winger grinned at the mostly symbolic attack. Then Stick caught him under the chin with the butt-end of his stick. The smile vanished and the player crumpled to the ice like a snot-soaked handkerchief.

A sharp whistle blast drew attention to the adolescent referee. The kid looked just as surprised as the adults that he'd blown it. Of course he had to – at the very least the unconscious mechanic was offsides.

I have to hand it to the kid, though – he had more stones than any of the players expected. He pointed a shaky finger at Stick.

"You," the kid said with as much authority his cracking voice could muster, "You're outta here."

Surprisingly, Stick didn't argue. He skated to the penalty box gate, entered it, put some plastic guards on his skates, then stomped out the back gate into the grandstands. A few seconds later he was standing with Jimmy, Stanley, and me.

"Took you long enough," Jimmy said.

Stick shook his head. "Yeah, the new guys wouldn't touch me and the fookin' kid wasn't calling anything."

I was a little slow on the uptake, but I realized that laying out his employee wasn't just a reflex; Stick did it on purpose. Staging a fight to get thrown out of a rec league hockey match seemed overly dramatic, even for Jimmy's crew.

I started to ask why ordering me playing security guard required such an elaborate meeting when Stanley's phone buzzed again. This time he smiled at the message on the screen. He looked at Stick and gave him a quick nod.

"New plan," he said to me. "Independence PD just spotted one of our stolen trucks near Fairmount Park. I need you to hook it and take it to Stick's garage. Get moving – we don't have the tow contract with Independence and I want it back before someone else impounds it. I'll text you the exact location as soon as I get it."

"Wha-...why me? Why not some of the other guys?" I stammered. "Or are they too busy playing games?"

Stick just shook his head at my taunt. Stanley replied for him.

"Everyone has a role. Besides, half the crew is too new to be trusted with this. Right now, your role is to retrieve our truck."

"And guard the safe?"

"Go to the university after you drop off the Escalade. Like I said, plans change."

"Your planning's been shit all day," I screamed in my head – but didn't dare utter out loud. Before I could think of something less likely to get me punched, my left earlobe tickled as if a furry paw batted at it. I turned reflexively but I didn't expect to find anything there. There was no danger, however I spied a new face among the spectators. Or rather a familiar old face. The ripped hippie who decked and cuffed me sat in the upper corner of the far grandstand with headphones covering his ears.

"Hey," I said, "Hot Jesus is here."

"What the hell are you talking about, ya puck bunny?" asked Stick derisively.

I rolled my eyes.

"The dude with the beard and ponytail who sucker punched me yesterday," I explained. I turned to Jimmy and Stanley. "Hot Jesus – you remember, right?"

They both frowned. I jerked my thumb to the stands. "He's

right up there." We all turned to where I had been looking. He was gone.

"Well, shit," I said, "he was just there."

They stared skeptically at me.

"He was! He was right over there listening to music," I protested without effect. "Aw, fuck it. Text me the damn address," I said then headed to the parking lot.

Chapter Nineteen

The hood of the old Ford pickup I'd parked beside was up. As I neared my truck I noticed a man in faded overalls and an orange stocking hat in the Classic Ford owner position: leaning over the grill staring at a silent engine.

"Hey," he said, "can you give me a jump?"

I hesitated, thinking I should help but knowing the ever-so-impatient Stanley would be furious if I didn't get to our abandoned Escalade right away. My dilemma seemed solved when I spotted on his cap the prancing pony logo of the Denver Broncos football team.

"Um, yeah, I don't think so, Donkey fan."

In retrospect, that's what I should have said. But, I wimped out.

My phone buzzed. I looked at it and confirmed it was Stanley texting me the Escalade's location.

I glanced at my own piece-of-shit truck, the driver's window still stuck half down, and knew there was an uncomfortably high likelihood it wouldn't start either.

I sighed and said "I guess so."

I popped open the hood of my truck then dug out an old set of jumper cables from behind the seat. I crossed my fingers while twisting my keyless ignition; the old Chevy hesitated, popped like a firecracker, and sputtered to a start.

The weather gods showered us with large, floofy snowflakes while he and I connected the batteries in our two trucks with the cables. The Broncos fan waited for his to charge a bit then cranked the engine. The old motor chugged and stopped. After sitting for another excruciatingly long minute, it started on the second try.

He thanked me profusely while I coiled the cables and closed my hood. He grabbed my shoulder as I hopped back into my truck, startling me almost as much as the broken seat spring jabbing me in the ass did.

"Hey," he said trying to hand me a wrinkled bill, "You didn't have to help – everyone's time is worth somethin'. Here's a twenty for your trouble."

It had only taken five minutes to help – hardly worth $20 and I didn't have time to chit-chat.

"Keep it. Help someone else out sometime," I said then shut my door. The guy gave me a quick wave. I nodded back as I figured a hero – albeit a reluctant one – should, then shifted into reverse. My truck's engine coughed and nearly died, reminding me I was no hero.

I stopped at the parking lot exit and reread Stanley's text. I wasn't familiar with the park but that didn't matter much; instead of sending me an address he sent me a set of GPS coordinates. I plugged them into my phone's navigation app and drove east while the program figured out the directions it would give me.

I was a couple of miles down Johnson Drive when my British-voiced navigator commenced ordering me around. She announced frequently in a clipped arrogance I find kind of sexy that she disapproved of the shortcuts I took and was "recalculating." After a couple of wrong turns near our destination I conceded that sometimes she knew best and reluctantly followed her instructions.

It was dark and snowing harder when I pulled up to the park entrance. I paused to rub my left cheek – the cold air and snow blowing through the partially open window scoured the side of my face raw.

Visibility was challenging and got even worse inside the park. Even without their leaves, the limbs of the dense stand of mature oak and cottonwood trees shielded me from the snow – however, they also blotted out most of the city's light pollution.

Idling along the narrow park road, I flipped a switch on the dash for the spotlights on the roof. Only one of the two came on. It flickered for a few seconds then burned out.

I sighed.

The nav app on my phone told me to go right, so I did. But it said I didn't go right enough. I turned three more times trying to get "right." I ended up back at the entrance but never saw our Escalade. Then I noticed an overgrown path a few dozen feet from the park road. The bossy Brit urged me to give it a try.

Two partially overgrown wheel ruts led to a chain-link fence. A large gate with faded "Danger" signs partially blocked my path. Beneath the slowly accumulating snow were tire tracks and arcing scrape marks through the frozen grass indicating the warning signs had recently been ignored. My uncanny skills of deduction – and the shrill voice on my cell phone – told me this was where my Escalade was hiding. The cops probably swung the gate shut to keep other nosey people away until their own service came out to retrieve the truck.

Ha, suckers.

As soon as I stepped outside my truck the snowfall got heavier. There wasn't any wind at all; it was like Zeus ripped open a pillow and dumped it on me. Or like I sat down on my sofa too hard.

I drug open the gate and rolled a few feet beyond the fence line. I found myself in a parking lot of the damned. Several rusting tanker trucks and old panel vans were parked haphazardly on crumbled asphalt. Everything was overwhelmed by years of unchecked weed growth. It looked as though their drivers Fred Flintstoned out of them at the quittin' time whistle thirty years ago and never returned.

A thin film of snow covered the actual tire marks but parallel paths of recently crushed weeds still showed the trail. I left the gate open and followed them inside. The tracks wound around a few of the old trucks, finally taking me to the crumpled fabric of another fence at the far end of the lot. My headlights swept across the backend of a new Cadillac Escalade nestled between a pair of dilapidated panel vans.

I parked near the Caddy and leaned over to check my glovebox for a flashlight. It was packed with unpaid parking tickets but no flashlight. The British woman in my cell phone announced cheerily, "You have arrived." The broken seat spring punched through the paper bags and bit me in the ass again.

"Hardly," I replied.

Chapter Twenty

Large snowflakes continued their lazy fall. It wasn't ideal weather to hook onto a truck but no wind and a balmy 33-degree temperature made conditions tolerable.

I backed my rig to the rear bumper of the Caddy. The rosy glow of my taillights and the muted rays from a distant streetlight struggled their way through the falling snow. I used to brag that I could hook a vehicle blindfolded. Surprisingly, that's not an effective pick up line. However, that was pretty much what I had to do this time.

Underneath the Caddy, the ground was dry. Dark and frozen – but at least dry. After a few minutes of fumbling around I had the cables and chains in place.

The snow swirled beyond the downed fence. I grinned at the rare bit of good luck, happy I finished the tough stuff just as the north wind picked up.

I winched the Escalade's rear wheels off the ground. I crawled back into the cab and covered the busted seat spring with a couple more Burger King bags then settled in behind the wheel.

I buckled the lap belt and popped the clutch. All four tires immediately lost traction and spun on the snowy grass-phalt. I frowned at my stupid mistake and clutched again, letting up on the pedal even more slowly. For an instant the tires threatened to spin again but I pushed on the clutch a little more until both trucks moved. My old rig surged forward so I let off the gas – and suffered self-induced whiplash when the Escalade's momentum slammed the SUV into my tow bar.

Even over the rumble of my engine I could hear the Caddy's plastic body molding crackle. I winced. It wasn't the end of the world; the truck was already banged up from its run-in with Nik's armored truck. Everyone would still bitch at me about the damage but Stick's guys could repair it easily enough – assuming his crew survived the rest of the hockey game.

My happy thoughts of Stick checked into the Plexiglas were interrupted by a loud clank.

Crap.

I got out of my truck again. Snowflakes swirled at the fence line but the breeze still wasn't noticeable. I didn't see anything that would have clanked on my side of the vehicles so I walked around my hood to check the other side. The source of the noise was obvious: the Escalade's driver's side door lay on the ground. I had a pretty fair idea that this Caddy was the one I handed off to Butch.

My suspicion was confirmed when Butch tumbled out of the truck onto the battered door. I took a few steps to give him a hand. As I neared I noticed his face was cut and bruised badly, like he'd successfully blocked several punches with his head. Duct-tape bound his hands behind his back and a red bandana filled his mouth.

136

"Mmph unh emph ehhh," he grunted to me.

Even after working several months with Stick and his crew, I still wasn't fluent in Canadian grunts.

"Huh?" I asked.

I took another step...and found an ice-filled pothole. My heel skated across the snowy surface, shifting my balance a little past the you're-falling-on-your-ass point. I thudded onto the ground a couple feet from Banged-Up Butch.

Behind the Caddy the snow swirled again. I finally realized though it wasn't because of the wind. Hot Jesus materialized through the flakes and hopped through a missing section of the fence. He ran across the slick ground like a snow leopard, stopping beside Butch.

He pointed at me and commanded, "Stay there." He reached for Butch but paused. He looked at me with a frown, his hand hovering over a cargo pocket I assumed held either his stun gun or more handcuffs.

"I mean it – don't fucking move."

Confused – and not wanting to get tazed again – I nodded in agreement and froze. Not literally froze – although it was snowing and it was feeling a bit colder – I mean I stopped fucking moving just like he told me.

He grabbed Butch roughly by his shoulder and jerked him onto his feet. Hot Jesus then flopped Butch ass-over-teakettle over a low spot in the fence. He hurdled it as well and vanished.

I waited a few seconds then pushed myself back onto my feet. I stood staring at the ineffective fence with my mouth open, still not understanding what exactly happened. Moments later a car door slammed. Then another car door slammed, quickly followed by the deep, guttural growl of a diesel engine roaring to life. What looked like two-dozen search lights came to life, bathing a large swath of the timber behind the fence with an almost daylight-like radiance. The mini sun began moving then rapidly bounced away from the lot. Seconds later the lights, Butch, and Hot Jesus were gone.

"Son of a bitch," was all I could think to say. It didn't matter: no one was left to listen.

Chapter Twenty-one

"I'm tellin' ya, Stanley, Hot Jesus fuckin' kidnapped Butch," I said into the Jimmy Phone. I was on my way to Stick's garage but figured I should report to my bosses what I'd seen before I forgot any of it.

"Why the hell would he want Butch?" he asked. Then he mumbled "I'm not sure even we want him."

I was on a particularly shitty stretch of 12th Street and hit a massive pothole, thumping my noggin on the roof of my truck. I hit the roof a second time when the Escalade bounced through the hole.

"Ouch. Dammit. How the hell should I know?" I snapped back at him. "He looked like someone used his face as a battering ram."

"Someone beat up Jesus? I thought you said this dude is ripped."

I hit another pothole and cracking my head on the roof again. Frustrated, I answered "Butch. Butch was beat up."

Without thinking I added "Moron."

The phone was silent for several seconds. "Did you call me a moron?"

"Wasn't supposed to be out loud," I muttered.

A few more excruciatingly silent seconds passed. "Stevens already reassigned his men," he said, thankfully ignoring my insubordination. "Dump the Escalade at Stick's and go straight to the university. Don't bother with the uniform bullshit, just get over there and keep people away from the safe."

"People? What *people*? I asked, getting a little more shrill than a normal man's testosterone should allow. "How do I stop *people*?"

"Just...anybody. Stop them with a bunch of stupid-ass questions and annoy them into leaving. You know – be yourself."

CLICK.

"Smartass," I muttered after double-checking the phone to make sure he really hung up and didn't hear that as well.

I drug the Escalade the rest of the way to the compound in the West Bottoms. Stick and his crew work in two massive gray sheet metal buildings centered in a huge gravel lot. Although I had keys for the gate, Stick has never entrusted me with keys to the buildings.

Ordinarily, the surrounding neighborhood is a bit sketchy at night and leaving an expensive SUV there would be like putting a Post-it with a note saying "Don't take me" onto a $100 bill and tossing it to the wind. However, the buildings and gravel lot are enclosed by a tall fence, lit better than most tanning beds and, most important, Stick and his goons have a reputation for dealing quite harshly with anyone who messes with their stuff. I felt pretty comfortable leaving the Caddy – even minus one of its doors – in the narrow space between the two buildings.

I was unhooked from the Escalade and back on the street in no time. During the fifteen-minute drive from Stick's to the school I passed the demolition project on Main Street. The site was lit up like a prison yard during a jailbreak, bustling with several workers in white overalls. There were even a few guys I recognized from Stick's crew standing watch at the gate. I figured Jimmy's schedule had to be pretty tight to pay night wages just to knock down an old building.

A few minutes later I finally rolled onto the grounds of the University of Missouri Kanas City. The students were still on Winter Break so traffic on the campus was light. I parked in a tow away zone near Kokafear Hall's front vestibule because, ya know, no one tows a tow truck.

Kokafear Hall is a very college-y looking building. It's a squat, three-story, brick and limestone structure that was probably several years old when cars were still started with a hand crank.

I walked inside the lobby and looked around, quickly finding that college buildings at night during a holiday break are quiet. Unsettlingly quiet. I also found that to save energy, only half the lights were on and the temperature hovered just north of 60 degrees. What I didn't find, however, was Doctor Benton.

I figured some archeological emergency suddenly popped up that couldn't wait another hour to be solved. I dropped my butt on a bench near the entrance and waited for the doctor. Fortunately, there were several bulletin boards on the wall, each plastered with dozens of photocopied flyers for club meetings, textbooks for sale, students seeking roommates, and high interest credit card applications. Unfortunately, I read every single item and Doctor Benton was still

MIA.

My butt got tired of sitting. I stood up and stuffed my hands into my pockets, glancing around for inspiration. The hallway extended the same distance to both my left and my right: a 50-50 proposition. I shrugged and shuffled off to the left.

The rubber soles of my boots squeaked with each step on the terrazzo floor. The annoying screeches bounced off the yellowed plaster walls, announcing my presence to the gods and everyone.

I peered through doorways into six classrooms before arriving at a fire exit at the end of the hall. All the rooms were dark and empty. Probably empty. I decided the doctor wouldn't be chilling in the dark and I had absolutely zero interest in meeting anyone who would hang out in an unlit classroom so I didn't investigate them further.

Coming up empty on the left wing, I headed back toward the lobby, hoping Doctor Benton was somewhere along the other hallway. The ache in my knee increased and I really didn't want to check all four floors of the building, particularly since the old building didn't appear to have any elevators.

The right side had only three doors irregularly spaced along the hallway. The first door opened onto a shallow ramp sloping into a stuffy, cavernous lecture hall filled with dozens of theater seats. At the bottom of the aisle was a podium in front of a spacious white board, both illuminated by a few can lights in the high ceiling. My eyes glazed over imagining the topics discussed in there. No sign of the doctor though.

The next room I checked was a computer lab. The lights were

off but I could see the room was empty from glowing monitors. I have to admit I was a tad disappointed the History Department screen savers weren't Flying Toasters.

The last door was just before the fire exit and stairway. I approached it with dread. I really, really didn't want to climb any stairs.

The door was closed. I opened it and looked into yet another cold, dark room. This one though, had a sunken floor. An Exit sign in the far corner cast several faint shadows toward me, hinting the space was a storeroom cluttered with junk. Still no doctor.

"Stairs it is, dammit," I muttered into the gloom.

My nose tickled like it was being touched by a furry paw. I brushed away the sensation and stepped toward the stairwell – and received a harder bop on the nose. I shook my head to clear away the phantom sensation. Mid shake I recognized one of the shadows in the store room; a large, rectangular safe-ish looking shadow.

It made sense: the safe in the secret room was large and looked extremely heavy. There was probably a service elevator somewhere but why take something like a big-ass iron safe to an upper level?

I looked back down the hallway to the lobby to make sure Doctor Benton hadn't returned while I was exploring. Seeing no one, I stepped through the storeroom door for a closer look.

Energy savings be damned, I knew there had to be a manual switch for the lights somewhere. I felt along the wall next to the doorframe and fumbled across a bank of switches. I flipped one, bringing to life a moveable work light hanging from the ceiling.

Below it, sitting on a low workbench, was the "Mystery of History" safe. On the floor below the workbench was the unmoving form of a petite woman in leather boots, jeans, and wool turtleneck sweater. I couldn't see her face but I certainly recognized the figure beneath the brown pony tail.

"Dea!"

Chapter Twenty-two

I didn't know how my girlfriend ended up at the university but I suspected the allure of that damned safe had a lot to do with it. Regardless, she was on the floor and not moving and that scared the hell out of me.

I rushed into the room to help. The toe of my boot snagged some loose weatherstripping on the door threshold. I banged my knee on the step below then thudded onto the floor, face to face with Dea.

Except it wasn't Dea.

Oh, the woman I faced looked a lot like my girlfriend – but it wasn't her. Her jaw was more square, her brow a bit more furrowed, and her eyes, which fluttered open while I was staring at her, were a deep blue bordering on purple.

Her eyes were open?

"AAAA!" she screamed.

"AAAA!" I responded.

I pushed myself up, sitting on the floor. She did the same.

"Who the hell are you?" she asked.

"I'm Hook. I'm here to guard the," I pointed to the safe which I noticed was open, "-the, uh safe."

She popped onto her feet with an ease I knew I was in no way going to duplicate. I rolled onto my knees, grabbed ahold of the workbench, and slowly pushed myself onto my feet.

She glanced at her smart watch and tapped it a few times. "Well, you're too late to be of any use."

I was flattered she thought there was a time I would have been of use. I stared at her, giving my infallible intuition a chance to get a read on her. She looked amazingly like Dea. Except for the chin – and the eyes which were glaring back at me. I sensed she was pissed.

"Dr. Benton, right?" I asked.

She looked at me sideways.

"Yes," she answered tentatively.

"Stanley sent me here to meet you."

At the mention of Stanley, she noticeably relaxed.

"Oh, ok then. I was just expecting someone larger," she said, then immediately reddened at the inadvertent insult.

"Er, right," I said, reddening as well. I changed the subject.

"What happened?"

"There were a couple of cops guarding the room but they got a call and had to leave." She frowned at the memory then continued with her story. "A few minutes after they left, two men in black ski masks came in. The idiots asked me what was in the safe. I said no one would know for days. They laughed and pushed me out of the way. One of them stuck a small metal box on the door then spun the dial several times until the lock clicked. They opened the door but only found a piece of paper inside. They got angry and yelled at each other, then yelled at me, accusing me of already opening it. One of them hit me on the chin. Then I saw you."

I crossed the room and faced the safe. A light metal frame and holding wires and a pair of servos surrounded it. It reminded me of the time I disassembled my toy remote control car and couldn't put it back together.

"What's all this stuff?" I asked.

"One of our Mathematics grad students asked to try one of her algorithms to crack the safe in less time than trying every possible combination. She thought it would take a few days instead of a couple weeks."

"Weeks?"

"Yes, it's a four-number lock – a hundred million possible combinations. Her theory was the combination was probably a date so she was going to have the servos randomly try combinations of one to twelve for the first number, one to thirty-one for the next, 18 or 19 for the third, and zero to 99 for the last. Sort of mixing psychology with math."

She saw me crunching numbers in my head.

"Literally one hundred million," she said again, shaking her head.

"Er, right," I stammered. "But, surely a good locksmith would be faster."

"Obviously," she said pointing to the open safe, "but James said there was no hurry and to let her try."

"James?"

She blushed. "Mr. Penders, I mean."

I sensed there was a really interesting story of Dr. Benton and *James* but I thought I'd save my questions about it for when I wasn't at a crime scene. The fact that Jimmy wasn't in a hurry to look inside seemed odd though.

"When did the men get here?" I asked.

She looked at her watch again. "I don't know, two hours ago maybe a little more."

Exponents aren't my strong suit but simple subtraction I can do. The missing Escalade was spotted not too long after that.

"What was on the paper they found?"

"I don't know. They tossed it over there," she said pointing to the workbench.

I picked up the piece of paper and was shocked with what it said. It was a yellowed, slightly brittle flyer for an event at Buffalo Bills – the upcoming Buffalo Bill's grand opening party on August 29, 1973.

I handed it to Dr. Benton. Her eyes grew big with surprise then shrank to slivers with suspicion. Whatever it was she was thinking, she kept it to herself. She handed the mysterious flyer back to me without saying a word. I folded the paper a couple of times and stuffed it in my front pocket.

"What'd you think would be inside?"

She sighed. "Of course, everyone has a theory. Personally, I thought the missing guns from the Union Station massacre would be in there. You know, kind of as an insurance policy to keep Pretty Boy

Floyd and his gang from turning stoolie."

I looked at the safe more closely. It certainly looked old. And it appeared very similar to what I remembered. But there was something about it that made me feel it wasn't the same safe I saw in the basement.

Dr. Benton stepped away and was on her phone describing the break in. Since she was talking to the cops I decided to call Stanley.

He answered the call with, "What's going on?"

"Hello to you, too, Stan," I said. I continued before he could reply. "When I got here the doctor was knocked out and the safe was open."

"Dammit," he said. "This is not what we wanted."

That was not at all what I expected to hear.

"Wha? We? Wanted what?" I jabbered.

He ignored my stuttering.

"Go home and wait for me to call. Fix the sight on your gun and load it."

CLICK.

Chapter Twenty-three

I waited with the doctor for the cops to show up. Jimmy arrived first. He brushed past me and went straight to Dr. Benton. They wrapped their arms around each other tightly. I'd characterize their embrace as far beyond cordial.

Jimmy and the doctor hugged one another for several moments, staring into each other's eyes and talking quietly. He carefully brushed away a strand of hair from her cheek. She blushed when she saw me watching them. My interest was piqued but the look Jimmy – James – shot me quashed the questions I had.

The cops walked in soon after the public display of affection ended. Jimmy looked at them with venom. The officers glanced at one another briefly, silently trying to decide who would talk to the attractive lady and who would have to deal with Jimmy. I assume the one who ultimately walked over to Dr. Benton had seniority or had won a recent bet. While he took a statement from the doctor, Jimmy escorted the other officer to the open safe.

Jimmy immediately tore into him for leaving the safe unguarded accenting his displeasure several times by jabbing a finger into the cop's body armor. When regular people touch a cop, they get cuffed and stuffed into the back seat of a cruiser. This officer obviously knew Jimmy, though, and merely nodded. He tried to explain the decision to leave came from higher up the chain of command. Of course, it did. I knew that and I knew Jimmy knew it, too. I had a feeling that although he was genuinely and rightly pissed, Jimmy was grandstanding a bit for the pretty doctor.

I felt a bit superfluous at that point. I waved for Jimmy's attention and shrugged at him when he looked at me. He waved me off then resumed berating the poor cop.

I walked back out to my truck. A parking ticket under the wiper blade rattled with the light breeze. I snatched it from the windshield and stuffed it into the glovebox with the others.

A few minutes later I finally rumbled back to the lot by my loft. It was full so I parked in a No Parking Zone on the street.

I carefully opened the front door this time, peering inside to make sure I didn't bounce off another neighbor. Thankfully, the Snooper Twins weren't still loitering in the lobby. I was able to grab my boxful of junk mail and get into the elevator without their tongue clucks and disapproving looks.

The elevator shuddered to a stop and dumped me onto my floor. I trudged to my door, fumbling the keys out of my pocket along the way. Before I could put the key in the lock, an excruciating piercing sensation in my hand stopped me. It was like two tiny fangs clamped onto the web between my thumb and forefinger. The pain was so sharp I dropped my keys.

It took me a couple of years to realize that Patch and I have a special connection. More special than just predicting when a phone will ring. I'll be damned if I know how it works; I've never asked him and he's never told me. I've never let anyone else in on our little secret either – people think I'm odd enough as it is.

Unfortunately, I don't always understand what Patch tells me. Except this time. This time it was crystal clear something was wrong – very wrong – in my home. I knew Patch wanted me to stay out. I couldn't, though. There was no way I would leave my little partner in danger.

I picked up my keys and carefully unlocked the door. I slowly pushed it open. It creaked like a cheesy haunted house casket.

"Come on in, Hook. We've been waiting for you," called out an all-too familiar voice.

Samantha, my crazy ex, was back.

Chapter Twenty-four

Even though Samantha obviously knew I was there, I still tiptoed into the loft. Patch was on the floor shaking, hiding behind the kitchen island. He looked at me like I was an idiot for being there. He was probably right. Dea was on the couch, hands behind her back; stony faced but with a combination of fear and anger in her eyes.

Samantha stood in front of Dea, her auburn hair a tangled mess. My eyes grew big when I saw she wore the all black garb of a small winter ninja. I absentmindedly rubbed the lump on my temple.

On closer inspection though, I noticed the black jeans and black shirt she wore were rumpled like she was coming off a multi-day bender. She looked frazzled. She lazily waved a snub-nosed revolver in my direction. Scratch that, she looked frazzled – and dangerous.

A pair of handcuffs lay on the coffee table beside her.

"Really, Sam? Cuffs again?" I asked.

"Oh, sweetie, of course. Your girl doesn't seem to like them as much as you do though," she said shaking her head sadly at Dea.

"Where is it, Hook?!" she barked abruptly. Her sudden change in tone took me by surprise.

"What the hell are you talking about?"

I left off the "you crazy bitch" as I figured that was implied.

"The safe. Where is the safe?" Her voice crept up in pitch, sounding even more unstable than usual.

"Damned if I know," I lied, then after a moment added, "you know, your old man told me just this morning that safe has ledgers of crooked cops and politicians. Are you trying to get back in Daddy's good graces by protecting the Assante name?"

"Ha!" she scoffed. "He's an idiot; thinks old family reputations matter. Everyone was on the take. And you know what? Nobody cared. Nobody!" she said even more shrilly. Her eyes sparkled. "That safe is full of gold," she added with a greedy smile.

Samantha wiped sweat from her forehead with the back of her gun hand. I ducked as the barrel swung past me.

"The Boss always said the safe contained gold and jewelry," she whispered, then looking at Dea, demanded loudly "Didn't he?"

Dea nodded slightly, "He said there was gold in the Library, but that's not what people think he-."

Sam cut off Dea's affirmation, instead shifting her focus to me.

"Where's the safe?" she demanded.

I stood wordless, no longer under that nutjob's spell.

"Hook, you've grown a spine," she said with impressed surprise then lowered her voice, "You are so hot to me right now."

She brushed her cheek to my cheek; her hot breath blowing into my ear. She pressed her lips to mine.

My throat was as dry as a straight gin martini.

"I saw you this morning. You were there – on the hook again. But, tell me, where did Penders hide that safe," she whispered.

Sure, I knew. I knew as soon as I saw the flyer for Buffalo Bill's grand opening where the safe was. It sure as hell wasn't with Dr. Benton at the university.

"At the university," I lied, my voice raspy.

Sam slapped me with the back of her hand then immediately softened. "The real safe," she cooed, "Please – they're going to hurt me. I need it, Hook. I need it bad."

I was thinking if I had a nickel for every time Sam said that to me...

She interrupted my count between zero and one with another kiss, a deep kiss with nearly believable passion. She tickled my tonsils then literally tongue-tied me with hers. She tasted like stale menthol and 80-proof desperation.

I wasn't about to let the crazy bitch manipulate me. Not again.

CLICK...CLICK

DAMMIT! She handcuffed me while I was steeling my resolve. As I berated myself for being so fucking stupid she shoved me onto the sofa next to Dea. More stuffing bellowed out from the bullet holes.

Patch hissed and rocketed across the room, leaping onto the back of the couch behind Dea. He hissed at Sam again and sprinted to the bedroom.

Dea's eyes blazed. Sam shifted her attention to Dea.

"Jealous, sweetie?"

Dea squirmed on the sofa.

"Hook," Samantha said to me, "you overachieved again." She turned back to Dea. "He's not good enough in bed to stay with unless you need something – what is it you want from him?"

"Hey!" I protested, "That's not...that's probably not true!"

Sam ignored me. She sat down on the couch beside Dea.

"Surely you know you can do better," she said, slowly running the back of her fingers down Dea's left cheek. She caressed her chin with a fingertip then glided the back of her fingers along the right cheek. Dea's eyes fluttered then closed. She sighed then lightly pressed into Sam's touch.

I was stunned by what I was seeing.

"You are pretty. Plain, but very pretty," Sam whispered. Dea nuzzled her hand.

My throat constricted, my mouth dropped open. Sam trailed a fingertip along Dea's jaw to under her chin. Dea raised her face to look into Sam's eyes. Sam lightly licked her lips and leaned in toward Dea, her lips just millimeters from Dea's.

Dea reached up and gently caressed Sam's cheek with the back of her left hand. Sam's lips parted slowly, her eyes glistening as her pupils dilated to the size of Minsky's extra-large pizzas.

I wondered if that was how I looked before Dea kissed me. Then it dawned on me that Dea's hand was free. That realization crossed Sam's thoughts about the same time as mine; Dea wasn't handcuffed any longer.

It was too late, though. The haymaker Dea threw caught Sam

right on the temple. The revolver exploded, putting a new hole in the couch between Dea and me. Samantha flopped onto the floor like an unwanted American Girl doll. The gun skittered across the floor and stopped in the center of the room.

My ears rang from the gunshot. Light gray smoke floated over the coffee table. I shifted to look at Dea. Some feathers puffed out of the newest bullet hole.

"How...wha...how?" I stammered.

Dea shrugged in response, pointing to her ears.

"How did you do that?!" I shouted to be heard over the ringing.

She smiled and held up one of Patch's favorite fetch toys: a small piece of ribbon with a tiny chrome handcuff key tied to it.

Chapter Twenty-five

Patch hopped onto Dea's lap and gave me a very smug – fuzzy – but smug look. He purred so loudly I could hear him over the slowly diminishing ringing in my ears. I moved closer so Dea could uncuff me. When she finished I leaned in and gave them both a relieved hug.

Patch, not appreciating our Hallmark moment, struggled free from the embrace and jumped onto the coffee table. He stood guard over the unconscious Samantha, his tail standing tall and fluffed out to the size of a beer keg.

When a known fugitive shoots a hole – scratch that – shoots *another* hole, in your sofa, the smart play is to call the cops. But Sam was asking a lot of questions about finding a safe that Jimmy obviously wanted kept unfound. I grabbed the Jimmy Phone and hit the emergency button that connected me to Stanley.

"Uh, Stan, we have a problem..."

"Hook? What the hell?" both he and Dea said simultaneously.

"What problem?" Stan asked.

"Why Stanley?" Dea demanded.

Two conversations were about one and a half more than I could handle at the time. I shot Dea a stern look. "Shoosh," I pleaded.

"You're shooshing me again?" Stanley grumped. "Next time I see you we are having a serious discussion about your recent attitude."

"Not you, I meant Dea," I said with a pleading look to Dea. She crossed her arms and mouthed the words "Call. The. Police."

There were a lot of voices in the background but I still heard Stanley sigh. "What's the problem?"

"Well, uh, Samantha is here in my loft. She was asking questions about the real safe. And she, uh, shot my couch again."

There was a lot of laughter on the other end but it wasn't Stanley's.

"You still there, Stan?"

"Real safe?" he finally asked.

"Yeah, she knew the one at the university was a fake. She said someone was going to hurt her if she didn't find the real one."

"Shit, this is sooner than we'd hoped. What did you tell her?"

I looked at the motionless Samantha on the floor. Patch waved a front paw in her direction, seemingly warning the unconscious ninja to stay down.

"Nothing. Dea knocked her ass out. She's still unconscious. What do you want us to do?"

"Good for Dea," he chuckled. "Stay put and don't let that bitch leave. And no cops. Not yet, anyway. We need to talk to her first."

CLICK.

Dea was glaring at me. I stood up and walked around the coffee table to retrieve Sam's revolver from the floor.

"We need to call the police," Dea said curtly.

"Stanley said to wait," I replied.

"That's ridiculous. She shot at us!"

Assante's words echoed through my head: "she could shoot the nuts off a mosquito by the time she was 10."

"It was an accident, just a muscle spasm from the punch. She wasn't really going to shoot anyone."

*Probably* wasn't – Assante wasn't the most trustworthy source.

I sat down on the sofa again with the revolver on my lap pointed more or less in Sam's direction.

"Now what?" Dea asked.

"Stanley said stay put so we wait."

She pursed her lips skeptically then picked up one of her history books. She flipped to a random page in the middle of it. Her eyes darted between the book and Samantha.

"That was, um, pretty cool how you decked her and stuff," I said, trying to bridge the silence.

Her eyes paused between the book and Samantha, landing on me. She bit her top lip for a moment then returned to reading.

I looked around the loft. Dirty clothes partially blocked the bedroom doorway. Teetering on my trashcan was a stack of empty delivery boxes from every downtown pizza shop. PlayStation game cartridges covered the floor in front of my television. And the books Dea leant me hid below the latest issues of Spider-man and Batman comic books. I glanced at the unsettlingly observant but still unconscious Samantha on the floor. Patch caught me looking at my ex-girlfriend and hissed again, reaffirming his unwavering disapproval of her. I shifted uncomfortably on the couch. It exhaled more feathers from the bullet holes. I suddenly felt very pathetic.

"So, uh, why uh, why do you stick around with, uh, me?" I asked as casually as I could muster while pointing my train wreck of an ex's gun at the floor.

Dea paused and looked at me again. She opened her mouth to answer.

A sharp knock at the door stopped her.

"Crap. Hold on. Stan's faster than I thought," I mumbled while hopping to my feet.

I stood up and jammed the revolver into the waistband of my jeans in the middle of my back. Patch continued his sentry duty over Samantha.

I opened the door expecting to see the hulking shape of Stanley filling the doorway. Instead I found an imposing Kansas City cop leveling his gun at me.

"Someone reported gunshots," he said sharply.

A large, floral mumu hovered behind the officer. Mrs. Sweeny's elfish head peered around his elbow, letting me know which snoop ratted us out. I wrinkled my nose.

Stanley said he wanted to talk to Samantha. I didn't like lying to someone who could have been a coworker but Stan also said no cops. I snuck a glance back at Sam. Fortunately, she fell facing away from the door and was partly concealed by the coffee table.

The officer squinted at me and added to his question. "Aren't you the dumbass who dated Lieutenant Assante's daughter?"

I frowned. We were never actually coworkers though and Sam only fired once.

"Gunshots? There haven't been gunshots here," I answered while scowling at my nosey neighbor. She silently replied by pointing to her eyes then to me.

The officer holstered his pistol. "What about her?" he asked, motioning to the still motionless Samantha.

"She, uh, tripped over my cat and fell. Happens all the time with the little scamp."

It was Patch's turn to glare at me. He hissed, too.

From the corner of my eye I saw Dea making faces at me for covering for the fugitive. I waved pleadingly at her from behind my back to knock it off.

The officer stepped inside the doorway. I shifted slightly to block him from coming any further. He stopped but still looked around me at the form on the floor.

"Ya know, she looks kinda familiar..."

"Well," I said, "she's a dancer at Bazookas. On the main pole on Tuesday nights – do you go there often?"

The cop blushed. Mrs. Sweeney turned her disapproving glare to the officer. She muttered "pervert" loud enough for everyone to hear.

"I, er, well, of course I, uh, don't go there," the cop stammered.

Samantha stirred, moaning lightly. Patch hissed and again raised a front paw, claws extended.

"See, she's fine. Thanks for your concern but we're ok," I said, trying to shut the door on him.

Sam slowly turned over, facing us. A trail of drool stuck to her cheek. The cop's eyes flickered as he figured out who was slowly sitting up.

"Hey!" he said in surprise.

The officer's yelp seemed to clear Samantha's head. She sprang to her feet. Patch swatted at her as she ran by him to the door. Mrs. Sweeney stepped past the cop to get a view of the commotion. Sam shoved the biddy into the cop, knocking them both down, then bolted for the stairs.

Mrs. Sweeney pinned the cop to the floor like a pro wrestler going for a three count. He rolled her off of his stomach and hopped onto his feet. He started after Sam but then seemed to think better of it. The cop returned to Mrs. Sweeney and helped her up – but accidentally grabbed a handful of her ample bosom in the process. She smacked him in the shoulder and called him a pervert again. He glared at Mrs. Sweeney, then at me. Noticing Dea for the first time, he touched the brim of his cap and nodded to her. He then sprinted down the hallway while jabbering into his radio that he'd spotted the fugitive, Samantha Assante.

Mrs. Sweeney smoothed out her mumu and took another look through the door. "Hmph," she huffed, tossing her nose into the air, then lumbered to the elevator.

Dea and I looked at each other in disbelief.

"What the hell just happened?" I asked.

Dea ignored my question. "We have to get to the impound lot!"

My jaw slackened as my brain sifted through the previous ten minutes. Sam saw me at the building towing a van. I told her I saw her father. She knew the safe at the university was a fake. I knew firsthand that Sam was a sociopathic bitch but no idiot. She had to have figured out the real safe was in the van I towed.

Aw, shit.

Chapter Twenty-six

"Grab your coat and meet me downstairs," Dea said, springing off the couch.

"What about Stanley?" I asked.

"We'll call him on the road."

I stopped at the kitchen and got Patch food and fresh water. He jumped onto the counter to supervise. I took the Kitty Krak box from the pantry and gave him a couple of treats, petting the top of his head until he purred. He munched on the treats as though he'd never eaten before. Then he rubbed his chin against my hand and purred. I skritched him behind his ears. He purred louder.

I noticed Dea watching from the doorway. I looked at her quizzically.

"That," she said.

"What?" I asked, not understanding.

"That," she said again, pointing at me still petting Patch. "That's why I stick with you," Without any other explanation she left for her apartment.

Patch rubbed against my hand. I scratched his chin a few more times then headed out.

I met Dea in the lobby. I looked at my faded tan Carhartt coat and clunky leather work boots and shook my head. I was the polar opposite of Dea's black field jacket, black cargo pants, dark hiking boots, and brown hair spilling out below a black stocking cap. She was dressed a lot like Samantha was only less disheveled. It dawned on me I don't know how to dress for stealth. And apparently, I have a thing for sexy ninjas.

Two police cars, lights blazing, were parked in front of our building. The cop Samantha bowled over and another officer gestured at one another wildly, talking as the snow continued to fall.

Dea and I looked at one another and silently agreed to avoid the cops. We walked down the hallway and left through a fire exit at the side of the building. We slunk over to my truck. Another parking ticket fluttered against the windshield. I crumpled it up and added it to the collection in the glove compartment then I popped the lock on the passenger door for Dea.

She tugged on it a few times before it creaked open. The odor to which I'd already become accustomed hit her like a club to the nose. She grimaced then hopped inside.

"What a piece of junk!"

At one time the old beast really had it where it counted but even I didn't believe it did anymore. I ignored the statement and turned the keyless ignition; the engine chugged twice then stopped. I turned the ignition again and only heard a rapid clicking sound from under the hood.

"Yep. Junk," she said again.

I jumped outside and popped open the hood. Clicking usually means loose battery cables or a low battery so I pushed on the heavily oxidized battery connectors to try to tighten them. I climbed back inside and turned the ignition. I didn't even get clicks.

"Battery must be dead," I groaned.

"Should we take my car?"

"It'll never be able to pull the van," I replied.

I beat my head on the steering wheel a couple of times, dreading the thought of calling Stanley to say I was stranded. Headlights from behind us lit up the still-open hood. An old Ford pickup stopped alongside us. The Denver Broncos fan driver peered through the passenger window and waved at me.

I got out of my truck to talk to him. We met at the front bumper.

"Need a jump? Must be sumthin in the air, huh?"

"Yeah," I answered sheepishly.

I got the cables out and a couple minutes later my truck chugged to a start.

"Thanks, uh, uh...?" I said, pausing for the Samaritan's name.

"Phil," he said, "Phil Karma."

My jaw dropped. Then he laughed showing off a few of his remaining teeth. "Naw, I'm shittin' ya. It's Phil Jones."

I chuckled along with him. "Good one. Call me Hook."

He put his hand out.

"Thanks a lot, Phil," I said shaking it.

His smile faltered.

"That'll be twenty bucks, Hook."

I chuckled again.

"Ha, ha. That's another good one."

He didn't laugh this time. "Everyone's time is worth somethin', ya know," he said looking from side to side. "No one else was gonna stop, either."

I saw Dea fidgeting as we'd already given Sam at least a ten-minute head start. I fished my wallet out of my pocket and gave the stinkin' Donkeys fan a crumpled Jackson.

The Samaritan-for-hire drove off as I slammed my hood shut, angry that karma bit me in the ass. I hopped back into my truck vowing to myself never to help anyone ever again.

I jammed the shifter into 1st gear. Dea looked annoyed.

"Can you call Stan and let him know what's up?" I asked.

She took out her phone and tapped its screen and put it to her ear. After several seconds of ringing the call dumped to Stanley's voicemail box. A bland voice droned, "Customer's mailbox is full" then disconnected the call.

We looked at each other and frowned.

"Well, I guess we go snag the van now then try to get ahold of Stan later," I said.

Dea nodded and put away her phone. The snow wasn't falling any faster but it hadn't lightened any either. There was a couple of inches of white slush on the streets that kept them mostly empty; we skated past Downtown seeing only Public Works snowplows and a handful of cars. Fifteen minutes later we pulled into the impound lot driveway.

I stopped at the office door. I asked Dea to stay in the truck. Nights are usually more laid back but I knew without towing in a vehicle or any paperwork I would have to do some pretty fast talking to get through the gate into the lot.

"I got this," I said with a lot more confidence than I had.

Dea nodded slowly and pulled out her phone.

"I'll try Stan again."

I went inside and found Officer Engstrom pulling a double-shift. She had her boots up on the desktop and was watching an old rerun of *Hawaii Five-0* on the television.

She looked away from the show long enough to see who I was then put her eyes back on the set.

"Why are you here?"

"I, um, have another drop-off. It's a—"

She reached under the desk. "Gate's open."

Grinning to myself at how easy that was, I skedaddled before she could change her mind. I jumped in and stood on the clutch then shifted into first while shutting the door.

The truck backfired as we chugged through the gate, the engine running even rougher than usual. We weaved and wheezed through several rows of abandoned and confiscated vehicles to space G-13.

"Who's Joe?" Dea asked, reading the side of the van.

"Some dead plumber. This is Dan's van now I guess," I answered with a slight shrug.

"Who's Dan?"

I suddenly understood why Stanley got irritated with me. Before I could provide another inconsequential answer the engine sputtered one last time and died.

"No, no, no, no, NO!" I pleaded.

"What's wrong?" Dea asked.

I looked at the dash. All the gauges looked normal. I turned the ignition. The engine turned over but wouldn't start.

"I don't know. Everything looks fine."

Then a distant memory of one of my old truck's quirks trudged its way through my melon.

"Aw, shit," I said out loud this time. I punched the dash. The lights behind the gauges flickered with several warning lights showing red. The radio burst to life, blasting a local sports call-in show. And, the gas gauge needle dropped from ¼ to below E.

"We're outta gas," I groaned.

Chapter Twenty-seven

"Now what?" Dea asked.

I thought for a moment. An idea came to mind. It wasn't the worst – or, unfortunately even the craziest – idea but it would solve a couple of problems. I opened my door.

"We're switching rides," I said. "C'mon."

Dea shouldered open her door and dropped out of the truck. I rooted through the random tools and trash behind the seat until I found a flat blade screwdriver and a pair of pliers. I reached under the seat, feeling around for several seconds before finding a Slim Jim. But a chunk of processed dried meat was of no use to us so I tossed it away. I reached back under the seat and finally found the flat, spring steel slim jim lockout tool I wanted.

When I turned around with the tools, Dea was staring at me.

"She had a pretty good lead. Where is she?" she asked.

It was a good question. I kinda forgot about her while I was searching for tools.

"I dunno. Maybe trying to find a tow truck of her own. Just the same, we should probably hurry," I answered, moving the tiny revolver from the middle of my back to my front waistband.

You can't be a tow truck driver without knowing a thing or two about unlocking cars. I wasn't very good at it but that didn't matter this time because old Ford trucks are some of the easiest in the world to pop open. I jammed the flat metal slim jim between the door glass and weather seal then moved it up and down a few times until it hooked the lock mechanism. I gave it a sharp tug...and felt a thirty-year-old plastic part break without unlocking the door.

"DAMMIT!"

I pulled the slim jim out of the door. As I moved around the front of the van toward the other side to try again, I heard the crash of shattering glass. When I got to the other side of the van, Dea dropped the tire iron from my truck and reached through the broken window to unlock the door.

"We don't have time for finesse," she said opening the door. I nodded vigorously in agreement.

We swept the glass off the seat. I climbed in and went to work on the steering column by prying off the plastic cover underneath it. I stuck the screwdriver into a maintenance release slot below the ignition and pulled out the key cylinder with the pliers. I wedged the screwdriver into the hole where the cylinder had been and gave it a twist. The engine churned slowly for a few moments and then popped to life. Things were finally turning our way.

My glee evaporated when I realized we had another problem. Although the van was running, we were boxed in by an old Honda Civic and rusted Chevy Cavalier parked on either side of it and a surprisingly new Mercedes sedan directly behind us. My stalled truck blocked our path out.

Of course it did.

The broken driver's door wouldn't open so I climbed out the passenger side to get out.

"Stay here," I said to Dea, "I'll knock it out of gear so we can nudge it out of the way."

The snowflakes seemed a little larger as I opened the door of my old tow truck. The wind picked up, swirling the flakes around like ice chips in a daiquiri blender.

I got into the tow truck one more time and knocked the gear shifter into neutral. My heart raced when the truck began to roll. It dropped back into its regular slow arrhythmia when the truck stopped after just a few inches.

The broken seat spring snagged my pants as I slid out of the cab, ripping most of the back pocket off the ass of my jeans. The unexpected ass-grab unbalanced me enough to take a knee in the 3 inches of wet snow covering the lot. Relishing the thought of bashing the old beast out of our path, I hopped up and kicked its door shut.

The thud of the rusty door slamming shut echoed dully throughout the lot. A few dozen feet to my right, what sounded like a box of loose silverware dropping onto the pavement responded.

I froze and tilted my head to listen. Another box of silverware hit the ground.

I realized after the second time, it wasn't flatware being tossed around. Someone was climbing over the chain-link fence.

Quicker on the uptake, Dea hopped into the van. She put it into gear while I jumped into the passenger seat.

"We gotta get out of here," I said, trying to ignore the barrel of the revolver digging into my hip. "Don't worry about damaging the tow truck, just–"

"Way ahead of you."

Dea rammed us into the side of the truck at an angle, starting it rolling. She tromped on the gas pedal causing the vans old rear tires to spin on the slippery surface. They melted through the snow quickly and churned on the parking lot asphalt.

I watched the side mirror while Dea slowly pushed the truck out of our way. I spotted two shadows winding through the rows of cars behind us.

"We have company coming," I warned.

Dea's face crinkled with frustration.

"Behind us?"

"They aren't yet but soon," I answered.

"They? Dammit. Let me know when they are," she said revving the engine.

I watched the shadows close on us. I glanced up. The tow truck moved excruciatingly slow and still blocked us in by a couple of feet. When I returned my attention to the mirror I saw the shapes dart behind the van.

"Shit! They're behind us!"

Dea hit the brakes, forced the shifter into Reverse, and stomped on the accelerator. We lurched backward a few feet, mashing into the Mercedes behind us. I kept my eyes on the mirror, looking for movement.

"Um, I don't see them now."

Dea didn't wait for results. She shifted back to Drive and hit the gas again. She angled us the opposite way this time. She bashed into the front fender of the Civic, easily shoving it the couple of feet we needed to get out.

As we scraped past the Honda, I felt the sensation of Patch's fangs digging into my right shoulder and shifted my attention to the window where the black ski-masked covered head of another winter ninja appeared.

"Gaah!"

The small eyeholes in the ski mask must have obscured the fact that the glass was gone but my yelp gave that away. I heard the door unlatch and thought to myself that relocking the door would have been a really super idea.

Reflexively, I threw a punch at the head. Instead of the knock-out blow I'd hoped to land, my knuckles slid across the itchy polyester ski mask. My thumb snagged the eye-hole and spun the mask around, completely blinding the bastard.

Dea's eyes widened when the door popped open about an inch; she jerked the steering wheel my direction. We bounced off the tow truck's rear bumper, slamming my door shut on the masked man's hand. I think it was a man anyways but based on the high-pitched scream it may have been a really large young girl. He dropped away, his scream lost in the sound of scraping metal.

After shedding the would-be car jacker, Dea straightened out the van and wove through the rows of impounded cars. I tugged the door shut and locked it. I checked the mirror. Two dark forms – one dangling his right arm – ran across the hoods of the cars, crossing diagonally through the lot to cut us off.

"They're gonna beat us to the gate," I said.

Dea glanced to the gate to our right and still a few rows of cars away from us. We approached an intersection in the lot, she cranked the wheel left. The rear wheels lost traction and we smashed into the grills of a couple of cars before she regained control. Both of our pursuers slipped and fell while trying to match our unexpected change of direction. I spotted something new: a dark pickup running along the fence line at the far side of the lot.

"They've got help on wheels now!"

Dea hit the accelerator again. She was smiling. Not a happy smile, but rather an ornery one.

"Hold on!" she shouted as we careened toward a narrow opening between two cars – an opening blocked by the lot's chain link fence.

"Oh, shit!"

Chapter Twenty-eight

The van fishtailed slightly as we gathered speed. Dea deftly adjusted the steering wheel with just her fingertips to counter the skid. I struggled to latch my lap belt, it's retractor locking up a couple of inches short each time I tried to jerk the buckle into place. I glanced at the cars and fence rapidly filling the windshield, took a deep breath, then slowly pulled the belt into place.

Dea floored the gas pedal. We scraped the side of the left car and smashed into the fence. It sounded like a whole goddamn store full of silverware exploded. A post bent under our bumper flattening the fence in front of us. I bounced my head off the dash as the galvanized steel net we'd hit interrupted our escape. The van pitched forward but we dangled about a foot above the ground, suspended by bent post and the metal fabric.

I checked the mirror. The shadowy thugs ran toward us. Dea gunned the engine but the rear wheels weren't touching anything. We rocked gently on the surprisingly strong fence. Dea looked at me, her ornery smirk replaced with helpless frustration.

I unbuckled my seat belt and timed the van's rocking. As the nose dipped, I pitched myself against the dash. Fists thudded on the rear door handle trying to force it open.

The post beneath us snapped. The fabric stretched further, allowing our van to finally touch the ground. A scream rattled the back door when the tires caught hold and launched us off the fence.

We jounced through a small ditch and onto a side road. Dea regained her stunt driver face, guiding our getaway van along the slippery pavement toward the sewage treatment plant. I leaned out the window to look for our would-be carjackers. The one with the mashed hand tried to run after us but tripped and fell into the ditch after crawling over the fence.

When I sat down back inside the van the back of my head was cold and matted with slushy snow. I shook it out like a common mongrel but some of the slush slid down my neck and back. The little revolver dug into my thigh, adding to the discomfort of the icy air blowing through the broken window.

Dea crinkled her nose at the overwhelming stench of frozen turds coming from the shit plant. "Where to?" she shouted over the whistling wind.

"Um, that way I guess," I said pointing toward Downtown.

Dea rolled her eyes at my overly vague directions but still turned right to take us in the direction I pointed. The Jimmy Phone buzzed in my pocket.

I fumbled it out and pressed the answer icon.

"Hello?"

"Vhere you at?" a thick East European accent asked.

"Nik?"

"Da. Vhere you at? Vhere iz goorl?" he responded.

"Girl? What girl?" I replied, confused both by Nik's question and the fact Nik was calling me on the Jimmy Phone.

"No more qvestionz from you," his normally calm voice sharp with irritation. "Vhere are you and vhere iz Zamantha?"

"Sam got away from us. We're in the van with the safe on Front Street."

"Anyone vollowing?"

"Well, there were two goons on foot but we ditched them. I saw a pickup too but I think we lost it," I replied.

The pickup rammed us. The two back doors separated slightly.

"Son of a bitch!" I shouted into the phone. "The pickup caught up to us!"

"Get rid ov pickup. Meet me at Steek's," Nik said as though ditching a tail was no big thing.

"What?! How the hell are we s'posed to—"

CLICK.

I looked at Dea. The pickup rammed us again, widening the gap between the back doors.

"He said to lose the pickup and get to Stick's," I explained. "I don't know how we're—"

"Stick's garage. Got it," Dea said as though losing a highly motivated tail was no big deal to her either. Her eyes brightened with excitement the way they did when we were 6 minutes away from somewhere and only had 5 minutes to get there.

I reconnected my seat belt, wondering how she knew where

Stick's garage was.

Dea floored it. The weight of the tools and safe over the rear axle kept the back tires glued to the slick pavement. The front tires, however, were quite a bit more squirrely. Dea navigated the slippery streets like a cross between an ice road trucker and a NASCAR driver.

Unfortunately, the shitheads chasing us were just as crazy-lucky. The pickup bumped us several more times as Dea wound us through the unplowed residential streets in Northeast Kansas City.

I tried dialing 9-1-1 but was placed on hold due to "high call volume related to the storm." I glanced at the large, fluffy flakes gently swirling in the breeze. I hung up on the soothing hold music with a colossal eye-roll.

Dea drove the van like she stole it which, technically, I guess we had. She broke nearly as many traffic laws as a Metro bus driver. The pickup continued to nudge us but she dodged and weaved, keeping them from getting beside or ahead of us.

Racing them to a tie, though, wasn't going to be good enough. Nik told us to lose them and I had a hunch our well-being depended on it.

They smashed into us again as we swerved onto the 4-lane Independence Avenue. One of the rear doors broke free and swung wildly with Dea's constant defensive swerving. I hoped it would shut itself with one of her swerves but the latch never seemed to catch.

As the door flapped open I thought I saw the passenger of the pickup leaning out the window pointing at us. The next time the door swung open I saw the passenger's hand flash; a bullet whizzed past me and put a hole through our windshield.

The unflappable Dea yelped.

"Fuck this," I said, disconnecting my seatbelt.

"Hook, what the hell are you doing?" she shouted as I climbed between the seats into the rear of the van.

The sidewalls of the van were lined with narrow shelves filled with tools and copper and plastic plumbing parts. Larger tools and iron fittings covered the floor around the safe. Keeping my back against the safe I waited for the sound of the back door slamming shut again to make my next move.

Another bullet whistled between the battered rear doors, ricocheting off the roof and into the dash. Dea shrieked and swerved, tossing me into a box of iron pipe couplings.

Not unsurprisingly, falling into a box of iron parts hurts like a son of a bitch.

"Ouch, dammit!"

"Sorry," Dea shouted, jerking the steering wheel again.

I rolled out of the pipe fittings box and crouched beside the safe. The rear door slapped shut for a moment. I crawled to the rear of the van and flattened myself against the side.

I pulled the revolver out of my waistband and waited for the door to swing open. Another gunshot zipped through the van, punching a small hole in the roof.

Dea cranked hard on the steering wheel, sliding us onto a side street. The rear door swung open, providing the passenger in the pursuing pickup a clear view into our van – and me a clear shot at their

6

We hit a pothole. My head bounced off the bare steel roof, the impact bringing stars to my eyes. I reached for the shelving on the sidewall to steady myself but instead grabbed the handle of a metal tool box. Dea swerved, knocking me off balance. My arms flailed as I tumbled backward. I managed to keep the revolver in my grasp but the much heavier toolbox slid out of my hand, hit the floor, and then bounced out the back of the van.

The pickup swerved just in time, narrowly missing the tool box. But the driver jerked the wheel to the left so suddenly that the asshole shooting at us fell out of the passenger window and summersaulted over the slushy pavement like a drunken gymnast performing a floor routine. I scored him with a 4.8, mostly for artistry. I'm sure Nik and the other Soviet judges all gave him a 10.0. The pickup swerved across the street and rear-ended a Prius parked along the curb.

I stuck the revolver into my front pocket then crawled back to the front of the van and lashed myself into the passenger seat. Dea made a bunch of turns, winding us through several residential blocks – she even idled through an apartment complex parking lot – until we were sure no one else was following.

She took us back onto the street and stopped for a red light. I snuck a glance at her. Her eyes sparkled and her cheeks glowed with the excitement like those nutjobs I see on the TV who throw themselves off buildings and mountains only to pull out a parachute right before they splat on the ground.

186

Or maybe it was just the glow of the red light on the traffic signal. Either way, I smiled at how lucky I was to have her and her craziness beside me.

Chapter Twenty-nine

The highway-style lights at Stick's compound were on, lighting up the yard better than the sun itself. I sighed with relief; the intense illumination and ominously tall fencing was a welcomed sanctuary. Only the stupidest of idiots would follow us there.

I opened the gate for us. We pulled into the gravel lot and skidded to a stop near the building closest to the main gate. I noted a second company Escalade was parked next to Butch's damaged SUV.

We sat in silence, slowly coming down from the chased-by-crazy-thieves high. I rubbed the right side of my face to try to stave off what felt like early onset frostbite. The snowflakes looked smaller and pelted the windshield like rice thrown at the end of a wedding ceremony. It wasn't just Dea's racecar driving that wind-burned my face; it was also getting colder.

"Now what?" Dea asked.

"We wait for Nik or Stan or...somebody."

She nodded and leaned back into her seat, closing her eyes. Moments later one of Stick's massive, bearded thugs walked out of the office door; he was one of the guys from the hockey rink. He stepped back inside for a few seconds then came outside with three other goons, all in dark jeans and black leather coats. He walked around to my side of the van.

"We've been waiting fer ya, ay," he said through the broken window. It sounded like Stick was hiring every fellow Canadian hooligan he possibly could.

"Where's Stanley?" I asked.

"Busy."

"Stick?"

"Busy, ay."

I sensed a trend but I asked anyway.

"How about Nik?"

"Also busy. We told him we'd take care of you."

I wasn't surprised by the response but I was surprised by the answer since Nik was the one who sent us there.

"We'll take it from here. Thanks." Nodding to a couple of the guys he added, "Robert, Douglas, unload the safe, ay."

Two large men walked over to the van and pried open the damaged rear doors. Dea and I looked at each other and climbed out as two goons crawled into the back. The van rocked as they wrestled with the heavy iron box.

We looked around at Stick's goons. They were all focused on the van and safe.

"Um, can we get a lift?" I asked the head thug.

He closed his eyes in frustration but then quickly reopened them with an overly friendly grin.

"Sure," he said turning to the remaining goon. "Seavers, take them back to the impound lot."

A groggy looking gorilla – the one Stick laid out at the hockey rink – scowled at him.

"Really, Justin?" he groaned.

"Just take care of them," Justin snapped back.

Seavers rolled his eyes. "'S go," he mumbled then shuffled off to the Escalades.

We followed. Half way to the truck Dea grabbed my sleeve and stopped me. Seavers, waiting by the driver's door, glared impatiently at us.

Dea disarmed him with her best fake smile. "Hook," she hissed to me through the fake grin, "I have a bad feeling about this."

I gave the grump a cheesy smile with less success; his grimace returned. "I know right?" I whispered back to Dea, "The dolt's concussed and probably half crocked on Mooseheads. But, we need a ride."

I resumed walking to the SUVs and our addle-brained chauffeur. When we were a few steps from the SUVs Dea whispered "How did he know we needed to go back to your truck?"

"Shhh," I replied, still grinning at Seavers. "Nik musta told him."

"You didn't tell Nik where the truck is."

I hesitated. "Nik's a sharp guy. Besides, Stanley has lojacks on all the vehicles."

"You really think they wasted a tracker on that piece of shit?" she asked, raising an eyebrow.

That hurt. Nobody should call my piece of shit a piece of shit but me. And she was probably right: no one would waste a tracker on my piece of shit.

Our driver snorted. "C'mon already, ay," he said tossing the key fob from hand to hand with impatience.

I nodded my head toward him. "Let's get out of here," I said.

Dea looked at me pleadingly, like she does when she wants me to understand after she's explained something for the bajillionth time.

The driver leaned against the SUV holding the key fob. As we got closer I noticed the side was heavily dented and its grill mangled. The Escalade looked an awful lot like it had been in an accident. Like an accident with an armored truck.

I paused for a moment then stepped forward.

"Trust me," I whispered. "Thanks a lot for the ride," I said to the goon. Then I grabbed the key fob from his hand and shoved my elbow up into his chin, driving him into the side of the Escalade. His head bounced off the fender and he collapsed onto the ground.

I looked over my shoulder and said, "Get in!" But I was speaking to thin air; Dea was already around the Escalade pulling open the passenger door.

I jumped in and immediately locked the doors. I pressed the starter button while buckling in.

"Ha," I said, "true keyless ignition."

The humor was lost on Dea. She didn't even crack a fake smile.

I threw the gear shifter into Reverse and backed us away from the building then drove casually to the gate. The goons were busy with the safe and the Escalade's windows were tinted to an illegal shade slightly darker than a black hole so I figured we were golden.

As we rolled past the van Justin raised his right hand and pointed a really large pistol at us. I wasn't too worried about that – I knew Jimmy's vehicles had bullet resistant glass. Apparently so did he. The hairy goon reached inside the building door with his other hand. My stomach twisted when he drew it back grasping a fistful of auburn hair. He shook his head at me and pulled the rest of a sobbing Samantha from the doorway.

"Dammit," Dea said.

We were only a dozen yards from the gate. My foot hovered over the gas pedal. But I knew we couldn't leave like this. I stopped the SUV in front of the gate and shifted it into Park.

"Dammit," I agreed.

Then I turned off the engine.

Chapter Thirty

We stared at Justin. I looked to Dea and said "Don't worry, we're ok in here."

The thug jammed the barrel of his pistol into Samantha's ribs. She doubled over in pain.

"Get oot here," he yelled at us.

I had the revolver in my pocket but I didn't see a way to use it without making our less-than-ideal situation even lesser-than-ideal. I left it be and hoped the gorillas were too preoccupied with the safe to think of frisking us.

I sighed. Our decision was made for us when a mangled black pickup turned off the street and parked between us and the gate. I hit the button on the armrest and unlocked our doors. Dea and I reluctantly exited the safety of the Escalade. Even though we weren't expressly told to, we shuffled to the front of our SUV with our hands raised shoulder high.

The snow changed to sleet, adding to our predicament by pelting us with jagged ice pellets. The two ass-munches who chased us from the impound lot got out of the pickup and joined the others.

Justin shoved Samantha toward us. She flailed her arms for

balance but fell whimpering to the icy gravel in front of us. Dea rolled her eyes and helped her to her feet.

"Corey," Justin barked while tucking his pistol into a holster inside his waistband. "Watch them."

The pickup passenger, who coincidentally looked as though he'd lost a tough fight with a concrete street, stepped in front of us. He rested his hand on the scuffed grip of a holstered .45 automatic.

Justin looked at his phone then nodded to the driver, "Corey, get in the van and help those hosers." Then he yelled at the van, "Hurry it up. We only gots aboot fifteen minutes, ay."

Dea and I looked at one another with raised eyebrows. Corey and Corey? That had to be confusing.

The other Corey looked familiar. I realized as he climbed into the van that he was the jackwad who hit me with the Escalade keys at Buffalo Bills. I flipped him the bird. Of course, he didn't see it since I only imagined flipping him off.

The van rocked violently, loud grunts accenting each jounce. A groan in three-part harmony was followed by the safe toppling out of the van and thudding onto the ground.

The safe landed on its back with the door facing the sky. Justin pulled a large iPod looking gadget from his pocket and set it on the door near the handle. He pushed the device's earbuds in his ears and slowly spun the safe's dial.

After about a minute he ripped the buds out of his ears and snatched up the gadget.

"This one gots different guts. I can't hear shit," he said,

stuffing the contraption back into his pocket.

He checked his phone then turned to Douglas.

"Get the hot-rod. And hurry, ay."

I suppressed a smile. I knew unless their hot rod had dynamite in its trunk they were screwed.

But instead of a souped-up car, Robert and Douglas rolled out a two-wheel dolly with a large green oxygen cylinder on it. A long rubber hose attached to the cylinder ended with a small diameter, 2-feet long steel tube.

My glee faltered.

The "hot-rod" they brought out was a special torch I'd once seen Stick use to cut through a truck axle. It sliced through the 3-inch hardened steel like a razorblade through a warm Twizzler.

Douglas ignited a handheld propane torch and touched it to the end of the steel tube while Robert twisted a knob on the green tank. Within seconds the end of the tube ignited and spewed a fountain of white-hot sparks like a Roman candle.

"Luminos," Dea mumbled.

"Wrong movie," I said as Robert moved the tube toward the safe. He plunged the oversized sparkler into the top of the safe like a doctor lancing a boil.

"Abra kafucking dabra," Justin shouted over the sizzling of the sleet vaporizing and the smoke of the torch cutting through the old steel. He moved closer to us to escape the shower of sparks.

My eyes watered from the icy sting of the sleet. Dea's did, too, but her expression told me she was genuinely upset.

"They're destroying the ledgers," she said, her eyes glassy.

Justin jerked his head around.

"Ledgers?!" He turned to Samantha with fury, "What the fuck?! You said we'd find gold and jewelry in there!"

He rested his hand on his pistol. "What gives, ay?"

"That's what Butch told me," she pleaded. "He said Jimmy told Stanley no one could imagine what was hidden in that room. *Pure gold.* That's what he called it: *Pure gold!*"

Dea stared at her feet shaking her head.

"Idiots," she mumbled.

I barely heard her over the torch. Unfortunately, so did Justin. "What?!"

Dea stared him in the eyes. "You're all idiots," she said acidly. "They didn't store gold in this safe, they stored information – information you're turning into ash."

Samantha looked frightened. If I could have seen me, I probably looked scared, too. She spoke up with a trembling voice, "She doesn't know shit. Penders is no idiot. He said gold. If it isn't valuable then he wouldn't have gone to all this trouble to hide the real safe."

Justin pulled his pistol from its holster.

"You'd better be right, ay." He glanced at his phone again and walked over to the safe.

"Five minutes! Move it!"

Robert raised a hand in reply, his thumb and index finger indicating he was almost finished. The thugs all moved closer to the safe, hypnotized by the torch's fountain of molten metal.

That was probably bad for their eyes but at least two of them held pistols so I figured fuck them; let 'em go blind. While they focused on the safe, I slowly lowered my hands. They were nearly to my waist – and the revolver in my front pocket – when a crash from the back of Stick's lot drowned out the sound of the torch and snapped the gang out of their trance.

"Seavers! Douglas! Go check that out! Corey, you go with them!"

Douglas and Seavers trotted across the lot toward the far building, clumsily pawing at their waists. The ass-hats may have been accustomed to carrying guns inside their waistbands but obviously never considered what a pain in the ass it is to draw them from under heavy coats, especially while running.

Corey, the pistol-toting drunken gymnast, started to follow them.

"Not you, idiot!" Justin shouted then turned to the other Corey. "You!"

Other Corey loped away. Our Corey pulled out his gun and turned to face Dea, Sam, and I. He waggled the barrel in my direction, motioning for me to raise my hands again.

Before I moved, gunfire to our right grabbed everyone but Robert's attention.

Nik's cab raced across the lot, rooster-tails of gravel flying from his rear tires. He swerved at the dumbfounded Douglas and slow-witted Seavers. His front fender nearly clipped them, forcing them to jump for cover behind Butch's doorless Escalade. The crazy old Commie swerved again, aiming his taxi at Other Corey. Other Corey sprinted to the corner of the garage and pressed himself against it.

The Corey guarding us turned his head to the commotion. Seeing Nik, he tried to draw a bead on the fishtailing Impala with his .45.

"Go!" I hissed to Dea.

Dea grabbed the shell-shocked Samantha by the arm and drug her around the Escalade.

I slowly stepped back from Corey's peripheral vision and aimed a punch at his jaw. Justin chose that moment to fire a shot at Nik. Corey shifted to the sound of the gunshot and my fist glanced off his sleeve. He jerked in surprise and recoiled his arm. My wrist got stuck between his forearm and bicep. Not only did I not knock him out, but I also garnered his full and undivided attention.

Justin fired again. Sparks flared from the hood of Nik's car. Nik changed direction again and aimed his cab at me. Well, probably not me specifically but rather Corey. At least that's what I choose to believe. Either way, considering our entanglement, if he ran down Corey, I was gonna be grill-grease as well.

I tugged my arm and quickly discovered that Corey was exceedingly strong when paralyzed by the sight of an oncoming Impala. I nearly pulled my arm out of its socket but was still trapped. Nik drew closer, his face peering between the bullets stuck in the thick glass. Our eyes locked. He grinned then the Rooskie prick gunned the engine.

Corey's eyes grew huge. I jerked my arm again as his feet churned over the icy gravel trying to scramble away. As we parted, the threadbare sleeve of my old Carhartt snagged the hammer on his pistol, flipping it out of his grasp. It tumbled across the lot about a dozen feet from us. He didn't care. Hell, I didn't either. He fell to a knee then half-crawled, half-ran toward Justin, the only gunman Nik hadn't targeted. I crouched and scrambled for cover behind the SUV.

Nik didn't follow him. Instead, he slid to a stop next to me, thumping his car's grill against the rear bumper of the SUV Dea and I tried drive away.

Justin was livid at the interruption. He fired a double-tap into the windshield of Nik's Impala. The slide of his gun locked open, its last round having been expended. The bullet resistant glass was pocked with several opaque white circles but didn't fail.

Justin hit a button on his gun, dropping the empty magazine from its grip. He reached to his waist and pulled out a fresh magazine. But Douglas, oblivious to the commotion behind him, finished cutting the hole. The thick chunk of metal fell free from the top of the safe.

Before Justin slammed the fresh magazine into his gun we learned Dea was right: the safe wasn't filled with gold but rather combustible paper. Its contents mixed with the fresh air and superheated metal shards and explosively vented with a small *whoomp*.

Chapter Thirty-one

Bits of paper blasted from the safe and fluttered around the compound. For a moment the only sound was the icy sleet pelting everything.

I looked to Dea. She was crouched behind the rear wheel of the Escalade. Samantha was pressed against the truck as well. The driver's door of the Impala swung open. Nik, still in his poofy Members Only coat and dress slacks, nonchalantly stepped out of the cab as though he was handing it off to a valet.

A gunshot skipped off the roof of his car. Unfazed he stepped around the open door and sauntered over to the SUV. He knelt beside Samantha.

"Pooch skrewed, nyet?" he asked,

Her eyes blazed. She opened her mouth to answer but before she tore into the crusty Commie, Jimmy, still in his insulated coat and jeans, tumbled out of the cab. He crawled along its hood to join us. Another shot rang out immediately followed by the CLANK of a bullet hitting Nik's car.

"Nik, for God's sake, get down and shut up, will ya?" Jimmy pleaded.

Nik shrugged and took a knee beside Dea.

Jimmy looked at me. "How many," he asked.

I ran through the faces in my memory: Justin the big asshole, the loopy Seavers, Robert and Douglas, Corey the gymnast, and the Other Corey which made a total of six.

Before I could respond Dea impatiently rolled her eyes and snapped, "Six. There's six."

"Er, right. Six," I echoed.

"And the safe?" he asked.

I pondered on how best to tell my boss – my alleged *mob boss* boss – that the safe he'd given me to hide was found and opened.

"Well, um, these guys – Stick's guys – um, they uh-"

"Oh, good grief," Dea interrupted, "the safe's open and the ledgers are destroyed."

Jimmy looked at her quizzically as a few scraps of singed paper skittered across the ground near us. He slowly nodded.

"I see."

Jimmy glanced at Samantha.

"Bit of a shitstorm you've created."

Her eyes flared again but for the first time in her life – the first time since I'd known her, anyways – she kept her trap shut. Instead she scowled and looked away.

"Nik?"

Nik poked his head between the bumpers of the Escalade and his car. He reached into his jacket and pulled out a Makarov pistol, its brown Bakelite grip and frame worn over the decades of its existence.

He stood with his head low, elbows pulled close to his chest, and gun extended with elbows bent slightly. He swept the gun through a 100-degree arc, firing four times, then calmly dropped back to a knee.

Nik nodded to Dea. "Da, siks, Bozz."

"Armed?" Jimmy asked.

Another shot thudded against the Escalade. Nik nodded and grinned in the affirmative.

Jimmy pursed his lips in thought.

"Let everyone go and you can have the safe! No one needs to get hurt!" Jimmy shouted.

Laughter drifted back.

"That you, Penders?" Justin shouted back. "Yer safe is worthless and that bitch still owes us."

Shots from several directions hit our vehicular wall.

Dea shook her head condescendingly at Samantha.

"What?" Sam spat. I thought Dea would punch her but instead she just bit her upper lip. Samantha turned away.

Jimmy looked up as if for divine intervention. When no lightning punched through the sleet he looked to the cabbie instead.

"Nik," he said, "back 'em up a bit."

Nik stood up and popped off a couple more rounds. He took a knee beside Jimmy.

"Only pyat now," the Rooskie said.

Jimmy stared back at him in confusion.

Nik eyes looked up and to the right as he struggled to find a different word.

"Don't know, Bozz. I only zee five."

"Dammit, Nik," Jimmy shouted, "I said *back them up*, not hit them!"

Nik looked insulted.

"Da, I mizzed," he replied, sadly shaking his head as though it pained him greatly to admit he hadn't shot anyone. "Vun eez gone though."

Jimmy's brow furrowed. Two more shots clanked into the Escalade. His brow furrowed further. I'd never seen my boss this flustered. Not even the last time someone was trying to kill us. Which reminded me that I really needed to talk to him about how much I hated the people-trying-to-kill me part of my job.

"Um, boss, we have a couple of armored vehicles here. Whadaya say we just drive off and let some cops talk to these a-holes?" I offered.

Dea nodded vigorously in agreement. Even Samantha looked to Jimmy expectantly.

"We could," Jimmy conceded. "But that doesn't solve the long-term problem," he finished looking directly at Samantha.

"Nik," he said again as Samantha looked away.

Nik crawled to the front of the Escalade then popped around its grill with the gun in his left hand he sprayed three quick shots toward the van then crawled back to us.

"Now chityri," he said holding up four fingers. Then pointing to himself and shaking his head innocently he added, "Nyet."

Jimmy chewed on the new bit of information.

"Here's a counteroffer," he yelled. "How about I fire you guys and give you a generous severance?"

Three rapid gunshots answered Jimmy's proposal.

"Hand over the bitch and we'll call it square," Justin shouted back.

Samantha shrank into the side of the SUV. Jimmy, Dea, and I stared at her. Nik closed his eyes, apparently meditating.

"Don't!" she pleaded. "I owe them a lot of money. Gold in the safe was my repayment." Then she whispered almost shamefully, "I think they'll kill me."

## Chapter Thirty-two

I rolled my eyes. It was the same overexaggerated bullshit I finally learned to recognize – a few months after she dumped me. I smiled to myself knowing Jimmy wouldn't be suckered by her.

"You're probably right," Jimmy agreed. He looked at his watch. Thinking out loud he added, "Stick and Stanley should be here soon."

The sleet turned to a light freezing mist, adding a clear slippery shell to everything. I shivered. So did Dea and Samantha. Jimmy and Nik looked unphased by the change, adding to my suspicion they really did have ice running through their veins.

"How much!" Jimmy shouted. "What's she owe?"

Another bullet ricocheted off the roof of Nik's car.

"Screw you, Penders!"

Jimmy looked at Samantha. "You really make an impression on people, don't you?"

Dea nodded vigorously but Sam ignored the question.

"Nik, take a look."

Nik snuck a look over his car. He held up three fingers and shrugged.

"Keep your eyes peeled – they may try to flank us," Jimmy said to us.

Flank? The only time I'd ever heard Jimmy say "flank" was when he ordered steak. He must have seen a war movie recently.

Jimmy glanced at my waist and quickly frowned.

"Is that a gun in your pocket?"

"No, Jimmy, I'm just happy to see you," is what I thought.

"Um, yeah," I mumbled instead.

"Doncha think you should have it out?"

I sighed with exasperation. "Dammit, Jimmy, I'm a tow truck driver, not a security guard!"

He jabbed me in the sweatshirt. "Then you shouldn't have worn a red shirt! Get it out and watch our back."

I freed the little revolver from the tangle of threads in my pocket. I flipped open the cylinder. The diminutive revolver only held five rounds – and Sam had already used one of them to shoot my sofa. Again.

I slapped the cylinder back into place and crawled to the front bumper of the Escalade. Nik took up post at the rear bumper of his cab.

The cold mist soaked my canvas coat. It froze making the material stiff. Dea and Jimmy whispered, oblivious to the curled-up Samantha beside them. It felt like we'd been there for hours; it had only been five minutes. I checked the street, hoping to see Stick or Stanley. Hell, even the cops would have been welcomed to the party but explaining everything might be tricky. However, nobody was there.

A shouting Justin interrupted my cavalry fantasy.

"Wha? Hey!"

We all looked at one another in confusion. Muffled grunts drifted through the saturated air. A shot rang out but this time nothing hit the SUV or the taxi.

Fast-moving footsteps scratched through the icy gravel. Of course they were toward me and not Nik. I cocked the hammer of the revolver, gritting my teeth with resolve not to let my shivering accidentally jerk the trigger. I crouched low; daggers of pain in my knees instantly requested me to sit instead. I ignored the ache and rested my shoulder against the front wheel to keep from toppling over.

When the steps sounded nearly on top of me, five tiny little razors dug into my left shin. It felt as though Patch was trying to sprint up my leg. I grabbed at the pain while successfully maintaining trigger discipline and not accidentally shooting a hole into the Escalade. Unfortunately, I lost my balance and tumbled onto the gravel in front of the SUV.

The revolver slipped from my grasp. I looked up to see where it landed just as Corey the Street Gymnast tried to step over me. His heavy biker boot caught my shoulder spinning me onto my stomach. His arms windmilled wildly as he struggled to stay on his feet. He failed spectacularly after a couple of comically uncoordinated steps and sprawled onto the gravel near his pickup.

More footfalls approached rapidly behind me. Having danced to this song already, this time I flattened myself against the gravel instead of rising up to look. I tensed, waiting for the inevitable kick. The ice-covered gravel further scorched my windburned cheek. The footsteps paused...then a pair of black combat boots landed with a thud inches in front of my face. I watched in amazement as Hot Jesus bounded over to Corey and hopped onto his back. He grabbed the clumsy thug's wrists and quickly cuffed them together with a large plastic zip-tie.

"Don't move and you won't get hurt," he said.

Corey swore, struggled, and even tried to bite Hot Jesus. I shook my head sadly knowing what was next: the Karma Fairy was about to visit and jam the Payback Wand up his ass.

Hot Jesus popped him on the noggin. He looked down on the unconscious Corey and added – quite unnecessarily – "I said don't move."

"Son of a bitch" was on the tip of my tongue but got lost somewhere. Nik strolled into view and pointed his old pistol at Hot Jesus.

"Don't moovf."

"Yeah," Dea said. "Don't move."

I looked up and saw her pointing Samantha's revolver at Hot Jesus.

"Son of a bitch," I stammered.

Found it.

Chapter Thirty-three

Hot Jesus slowly raised his hands but kept his knee firmly in the middle of Corey's back. Jimmy hopped up and disappeared around the trunk of the Impala. I looked nervously at Dea and Nik while they kept their guns trained on a rather calm looking Hot Jesus. About a minute later Jimmy returned.

"It's ok," he said with a nod.

Nik holstered his pistol and walked back to his car. He leaned against the fender and folded his arms. Dea lowered the revolver and stuck it in her jacket pocket.

"Why don't you come over here?" Jimmy said to Hot Jesus in a tone that was more command than question. Hot Jesus stood up and carefully walked over to face Jimmy. Dea watched every step. I looked away and scowled – and saw that Samantha was salivating over him, too.

"The other five are all unconscious and cuffed as well," Jimmy said. "If you have help out there you might want to tell me now before–," he paused, looking at Nik but pointing at me, "–before they trip over someone and get hurt."

Hot Jesus smiled. He reached into a small pocket on his cargo pants. Nik perked up at the move. However, instead of a weapon, Hot Jesus merely retrieved a business card.

"No," he said handing Jimmy the card, "I work alone."

Jimmy examined the card. "Luke Blackwater, Fugitive Recovery," he read aloud.

I snickered at the obviously fake name. Luke stared the chuckles out of me. If Hot Jesus the Bounty Hunter wanted to be known as "Luke" so be it.

An obnoxiously large Mercedes SUV skidded to a stop on the street. The passenger door opened. Stanley, wearing a black topcoat and black dress pants instead of his usual Adidas track suit, climbed out. I squinted to see through the fence and watched as he bumped fists with local football hero, Handz Middlebrook. Stanley trotted stiffly over to us as the Mercedes zipped away. When he got closer I realized he wasn't just wearing dress pants, he was in a full-fledged tuxedo.

"Date night?" I chided.

"Fuck you," he said to me like it was our usual greeting. Then eyeing Luke, he turned to Jimmy and asked, "This is our problem?"

Luke looked offended by the question.

"Most of the solution, actually," Jimmy answered.

Yet another black Cadillac Escalade arrived before Jimmy could explain. This one squeezed through the gate past the pickup and drove up to the closest garage. All of its doors opened and five guys got out. Four of them stayed with the SUV while the fifth, Stick, wearing only a sweatshirt and jeans, strode over to us. I shivered on his behalf.

"We're done at the Library, ay," he informed Jimmy. Then, nodding to Luke, "This our hockey fan?"

Luke started to talk but Jimmy answered for him.

"Luke is a bounty hunter." Then he turned to Luke. "You've been tailing Hook to find these guys?"

He shrugged away the question with a grin. Jimmy didn't pursue an answer, instead refocusing his attention on Stick.

"Apparently, your new guys are wanted in..." his voice trailed off, waiting for Luke to help answer.

"Wanted in Duluth. They skipped their trial for burglarizing a few jewelry stores," the former deity finished.

Jimmy looked away and grimaced. Obviously upset, he clenched his jaw then snapped at Stick, "We'll talk about the loyalties of your crew later. You guys clean up the van before help arrives."

Stick wasn't used to being talked to like...well, like *I* usually am. He walked away like a scolded puppy.

Luke seemed embarrassed for him but spoke up anyway. "I believe there's a price for her as well," he said pointing to Samantha.

Sam pressed herself into the side of the Escalade trying to disappear. Her eyes darted between Jimmy and me for help.

"Sure," Dea chirped, "you can have–"

Jimmy raised a hand. "No, not that one, we'll take care of her."

He and Luke locked eyes for a moment. Samantha was demonstrably relieved when Luke broke his gaze and shrugged.

"Ok. I'll be right back."

He jogged off the compound and down the block. Stick's guys wheeled out a hydraulic engine-puller hoist and picked up the safe. They lifted it a few inches off the ground then swore vociferously as they forced the overloaded contraption over the icy gravel back into the garage.

The bounty hunter returned in a white, 4-door Land Rover. The boxy old truck was covered in a shit-ton of aftermarket spotlights and its diesel engine whined like some performance tweaks had been made to it. He parked between the two buildings. The diesel engine continued chugging while he piled the unconscious fugitives inside it.

The freezing rain stopped but the wind picked up. I wrinkled my nose at the crappy aroma from the shit-plant next door then sat down against the front tire. I rubbed my sore shoulder and wished I still had some Vicodin left from my last hospital stay. Dea plopped down next to me, silently watching everyone work. Some scorched papers from the safe tumbled across the gravel and stopped against my leg. Dea reached over me and picked them up just as Hot Jesus, er, Luke, walked over to Corey. Her eyes grew huge.

Luke paused then came back to us and crouched down next to me. Dea quickly stuffed the paper into her pocket.

"Here," he said, fishing around in one of his pockets. He handed me a small white plastic tube. "Have some Ranger Candy. It'll help with that shoulder."

"Thank you," Dea answered for me, beaming a smile at him way friendlier than the stinkin' bounty hunter deserved.

I rolled my eyes. Even though I had just wished for Vicodin, I handed the vial back to him.

"Thanks, but McGruff taught me I should just say no."

He shook his head and held out the vial again. "It's just ibuprofen you idiot."

My face reddened. "Oh. Well, uh, thanks. I take that stuff like, er, candy."

I reached for the pills, snagging my sleeve on the mangled SUV bumper. My jacket tore when I snatched the plastic vial from his hand.

Luke chuckled. "Dude, you sure get hooked on stuff a lot. What's your name anyway?"

"People call me Hook."

He chuckled again. "Of course they do."

Despite knocking me senseless I decided Luke maybe wasn't so awful. After all, he did sort of save our bacon.

"So," Dea said like a giddy teenager, "Bounty hunter, huh?"

"Yep," he replied with a wink. "What's your name, angel?"

"Dea," she giggled.

Nope. I was wrong – he was definitely an awful piece of rat shit. I was not a fan of Luke.

"You know, I'm a little tired of this tow truck driver gig," I interjected. "Maybe I'll give that bounty hunter thing a try."

Luke looked at me like I'd punched him in the giblets. Then he laughed way too long and way too loud. "Ya know, I followed you for two days. You managed to draw out every one of these guys with your stupid luck. But a klutz like you a skip-tracer?" he said, laughing even more. "Only if you move to New Jersey."

"I ain't moving to Jersey," I snapped.

Luke laughed again then stood up. He walked back to the unconscious Corey and tossed him over his shoulder far too easily for my pride to accept sitting down. I grabbed the top of the tire and pulled myself onto my feet.

"Hook," he said.

I looked to him while clenching my jaw to stifle a groan as my back spasmed again.

"You owe me a pair of handcuffs."

My brain sent the words "Go fuck yourself" to my mouth but before my balls gave me permission to insult the massive bounty hunter he spoke again.

"Hey, I'm just kiddin'. Take care, you two," he said, smiling and winking at Dea again. Then he effortlessly carried Corey to his truck. He tossed him inside with the others then with a wave to no one in particular, Luke the Bounty Hunter climbed inside and roared away over the back gate.

"Good riddance," I mumbled.

Chapter Thirty-four

A navy Dodge Charger police car rolled slowly down the street. Red and blue lights in its grill strobed, giving the icy neighborhood a Christmassy vibe. It passed the departing bounty hunter just outside the compound. The freezing rain switched back to light snow adding to the holiday feeling.

Except Christmas had passed and the po-po was probably about to ask some uncomfortable questions.

Jimmy looked at the shot-up windshield of Nik's cab and shook his head. "Stick!" Jimmy shouted. "Your car in there?"

Stick, standing near the van nodded. "In the other garage, ay." He stuffed his hand into his pocket and pulled out some keys, tossing them in a high arc. Jimmy reached up with his right hand and plucked them out of the air.

He handed the keys to Nik then pointed to Samantha.

"She can't be here. Time to disappear."

Nik nodded. He put his hand out to Sam and pulled her onto her feet.

"Nik, wait," Jimmy said while studying the bullet-ridden taxi. "Take your go-bag – we don't need them finding it when they impound your car."

"Da," was all the rooskie said. He let go of Samantha and went to the trunk of his cab. He popped it open and pulled out a large duffel bag then reclosed the trunk. He returned to Sam and grabbed her by the wrist.

"Come vith me," he said.

My emergency kit is a grocery sack with a bottle of water, a box of Snickers bars, and a deck of cards. As Nik drug Sam toward the far building I pondered what necessities he kept handy.

Samantha's walk wavered between trotting to get away from the rest of us to reluctance in following the old taxi driver. But Nik never relaxed his grip. They reached the door just as the cop car pulled into the compound and stopped beside the pickup.

Sgt. Stevens stepped out of the car. He looked at us and sighed like he had a huge headache. Or like we added to his already huge headache. Either way he looked as though he really didn't want to be there. That was good 'cause I really wished he wasn't there either.

He carefully walked over to us, his head swiveling around as he studied the entire scene. He stopped between Jimmy and Stanley. They didn't speak so he did.

"Was that Sam Assante?" Stevens asked.

"That was Nik Andropov," Stanley answered.

Stevens rephrased his question.

"Was that Sam Assante with Nik Andropov?"

"Ya know, I really can't say for sure," Jimmy conceded.

"It's hard to tell in this snow," Stanley added unhelpfully.

Stevens opened his mouth but closed it without saying anything. He opened it again...and again closed it wordlessly. He looked at the far building that Nik and Sam had entered then he looked at Jimmy. He glanced at the taxi, double taking when he saw its windshield.

"Are those bullet holes in the windshield?!"

"Bullet *holes*? No," Jimmy replied. "That's some new bullet resistant glass Stick installed. We just got done testing it. It passed pretty impressively, don't you think?"

Jimmy was shading the truth just a bit. Stevens knew it and was visibly irritated. He tried a different tack.

"Who was that in the truck?" he asked.

"A friend hauling off some garbage," Jimmy answered quickly.

"Garbage? In a Land Rover?" Stevens asked incredulously.

"It had a lot of salvage value," I chimed in.

"Shut up!" Jimmy, Stanley, and Stevens said simultaneously.

"He's really good at it," Jimmy added. Then he folded his arms as if he was ready to go all night not really answering the questions.

Stevens shifted his weight from one leg to the other then put his hands on his hips. He mouthed several expletives that his professionalism prevented him from saying out loud.

"Goddammit, Jimmy, quit jerking me around," he snapped unprofessionally. He waggled a finger in Jimmy's face but a squad car, rollers on top blazing, slid through the gate and thumped to a stop against the rear bumper of Sgt. Stevens' car.

Stevens shook his head as Officer Thomas Flank jumped out. Flank covered his gun with his hands to keep it from flopping around as he trotted over to us.

"I've got a report of thoth fired," he lisped excitedly to Jimmy.

He noticed me and added "Oh, hiya Hook."

I nodded a silent "hello" back to him.

"Yeah, sorry about that," Jimmy said. "the guys set off some fireworks for New Year's."

Stevens rolled his eyes. Officer Flank's face crinkled up in confusion.

"But New Year'th ith day after tomorrow."

"Right. Canadian New Year, I meant."

"Oh," said a still confused Flank.

"That's your story? Canadian New Year's fireworks?" an exasperated Stevens asked. He swept his arm around the yard at the damaged pickup and Escalades, the bullet-riddled Impala, and the old plumber's van he'd sent to the impound lot not even a day earlier.

"Fireworks?" he asked again, turning to Stanley.

Before anyone could offer up a more plausible fib, one of the overhead doors on the far building opened. Stick's blacked-out Subaru backed out. The driver's window rolled down. Nik gave Jimmy a wave then put the window back up. The garage door descended as Nik roared out of the lot around the mangled back gate.

A dirty red taxi eased to a stop on the street. The driver's door creaked open letting out a small plume of light gray smoke. A rasta hat with Terry's goofy mug below it rose above the door.

"Somebody called a cab?" he asked slowly. Then he pointed to me and added "Hey, I know you."

"You're gonna need to fix that gate," Jimmy said to Stick over the roar of the car darting into an alley between the buildings across the street.

Stick opened his mouth to reply but was drowned out by a thunderous explosion in the alley. The ground below our feet quaked from the blast.

We all stared at the black smoke billowing above the streetlights. The orange glow of flames lit up the building walls. Stick's men grabbed fire extinguishers from the buildings and sprinted across the lot to the alley. Flank one hand on his gun, the other holding his radio to his mouth calling for assistance, galloped along behind them.

Terry let out an incredulous "whoa!"

I gulped. My stomach felt like I'd swallowed a brick. Distraught and shaking, Dea put her hand to her mouth. I wrapped my arm around her, pulling her into my chest.

"Oh, god. Not Nik," she whispered.

Chapter Thirty-five

We all looked in disbelief as smoking sheet metal rained down on the street. Jimmy pursed his lips and stared at his shoes. Stanley, the toughest man I've ever met, turned away, his eyes glossy and unfocused. Stevens looked angry and confused; he seethed quietly with his hands on his hips.

Officer Flank stood at the street corner talking into his radio. Stick's men reappeared from the alley. No longer carrying fire extinguishers and their heads low, they slowly walked back to the compound. The brick walls of the buildings behind them continued flickering orange from the fire they weren't able to put out. The lead man shook his head at us.

"I'll kill 'em," Stick growled. "They came after me and killed my friend. I'll fookin' kill 'em.

Steven's patience snapped. "Them? Who the fuck is them?!" He looked around at all of us for an answer. I didn't think it was my place to explain that "them" was a group of Canadian jewel thieves somehow connected to Samantha who stole Jimmy's old safe but were now headed back to Duluth with a bounty hunter named Luke who looked remarkably like an iron-pumping Jesus. Fortunately, Jimmy answered instead.

"We had to fire some of our mechanics. They didn't take it well."

Stevens exploded. "Didn't take it well?! Are you fucking kidding?! They blew up a goddamned car and killed Nik Andropov." Then he turned white as the light snow that had resumed. "Oh, fuck. Was Samantha with him?" he asked quietly.

Jimmy's words echoed in my head: *She can't be here.* We all looked at our feet in response.

Stevens stomped back to his cruiser. He opened the door and sat down, his feet still outside the car. He put his head in his hands and rested his elbows on his knees.

Stick turned and strode toward his men.

"Stick," Jimmy said sharply, "You do nothing."

Stick glared defiantly back at Jimmy.

"I mean it. Nothing without my ok. Got it?"

Stick continued to glare but nodded curtly. Then he huddled with his men near the van.

I looked back to Stevens; he'd watched the whole exchange between Stick and Jimmy and looked very interested. He reached to his dash and came up with the mic to his radio. He talked into it as sirens echoed through the neighborhood.

A Kansas City Fire Department pumper rig followed closely by a larger ladder truck roared down the street. Flank directed the arriving trucks to the alley. The firemen were connecting hoses to a hydrant when a wailing ambulance arrived. It parked near the alley and idled while the fire guys did their thing.

It was all very surreal. Jimmy, Stanley, Dea, and I silently watched the firemen open the nozzles and direct ice-cold water into the alley. Tears trickled down Dea's cheeks, freezing near her chin. I pulled her closer.

Jimmy looked at Stevens. Stevens, who had switched to his cell phone, glowered back at Jimmy.

"Ok," Jimmy said, breaking the silence. "Time for you guys to go."

My heart skipped a thump. The last people who had to go ended up in pieces. Lots and lots of tiny, charbroiled pieces. I wanted to voice my concern but the ever-practical Dea dove in first.

"Go?" Dea asked. "Don't you think they'll want to question us?"

"Oh, I know they'll have questions," Jimmy said, his eyes glued to Stevens. "All the more reason to leave until I have answers for you to give them." He looked up the street. A news van rolled to a stop beside the ambulance. A short woman in an insulated trench coat hopped out and quickly set up a camera at the end of the alley. Flank slowly backed away, trying not to draw attention to himself, then walked toward us.

"Yeah, it's definitely time. Go with Terry," he said pointing to the dingy cab with the dingier driver. "Stanley, you too. Ghost until I call."

Stanley furrowed his brow for a moment then accepted the order without question. Stanley put his arm in front of Dea and me, blocking our path to the taxi. "Wait," he said.

Jimmy walked to Sgt. Stevens' car and stood where Stevens would have to look away from Terry. Jimmy said something and immediately had Stevens in his face yelling at him.

"Now," Stanley said then quickly shuttled us to the cab.

Stanley climbed into the front seat. Terry opened the rear door for Dea and quickly closed it after she got in, forcing me to go around to the other side of the car. I let myself inside as Terry flopped behind the steering wheel.

Terry's cab may have had the same company logo on the doors but it was the antithesis of Nik's. It looked as though it hadn't been washed in months. The vinyl seats were cracked and had foam poking through like spongey hernias. The formerly maroon door panels were faded to a light gray and had holes from people kicking them. And the whole car reeked of ganja and Taco Johns; the little black pine tree dangling from the rearview mirror was obviously for appearances because it wasn't freshening jack-fuck. Bouncy reggae music hissed through a pair of in-dash speakers.

I slowly shook my head, worried I was departing for the last ride of my life in the shittiest taxi in Kansas City. Dea squeezed my hand, probably thinking the same thing.

"Where to, dudes and dudette?" our mellow cabbie asked.

Stanley answered before I could give the address for the Western Auto Lofts.

"Take us to the airport."

Chapter Thirty-six

Nik's loss was like a gut-punch and we were responding by going on a freaking vacation.

"Airport?! We are NOT going to the damn airport!" I protested very strongly in my mind. Dea needlessly shot me a warning look as though she thought I might actually pop off to Stanley.

"Stanley, where, um, where are we ah, flying to?" I asked instead.

"Jimmy told us to ghost so we're gonna just drive for a while," he replied.

"Ghost," Terry said. "Way cool, Stan-man."

Stanley rolled his eyes.

"Terry, just drive."

Terry mimed zipping his lips. He started the car and pulled onto the street. Jimmy's diversion worked: Stevens noticed too late that we were in the car. He ran after us for a few dozen feet before wheezing to a stop. I made a mental note to suggest more cardio workouts to him the next time I saw him.

We took a left onto Wyoming Street just as another squad car and two more news trucks arrived. Ghosting suddenly seemed like a great idea.

Stanley watched the side mirror for a few blocks, not relaxing into the seat until we cleared the West Bottoms and merged onto northbound Interstate 29. Traffic, like the falling snow, was light. I glanced at my watch thinking dawn had to be nearing; it wasn't even midnight. Still, I worried about Patch; he is a very cranky kitty when he doesn't get his 10 o'clock Kitty Krak treats.

Terry, unsurprisingly, drove as though he was paid by the second. A snowplow even passed us on the exit from Downtown. I figured the typical 25-minute drive to the airport would take just under half a lifetime on this trip.

Dea sighed, rolling her eyes in frustration at being part of the slowest getaway not made by a Ford Bronco.

"Stan, what's going on?" she asked.

"We are taking a short break," he responded matter-of-factly.

That sounded good to me. It wasn't good enough for Dea.

"Break from what?"

"The current situation," Stanley answered in a slightly annoyed tone.

I'd misread my girlfriend. Again. Her typically unbreakable spirit was, well, it was nearly broken. She was the one who popped off at Stanley.

"Dammit, Stanley! Either you tell me what the situation is – the *whole* situation – or I'm jumping out of the car!"

"Oh, no! Don't do that! At this speed you may stub your toe!" I mumbled under my breath.

Dea and Stanley apparently have bionic hearing.

"Shut it, Hook!" they said in unison.

"Seriously, what's going on?" Dea asked him again.

"No! You don't ask questions!" he snapped so sharply even Terry perked up.

Dea, still shaking with anger and probably a strong dose of residual fear, didn't back down. She shook her head dismissively.

"You didn't know, did you?" she asked incredulously. "You didn't know what was in the safe, you didn't know about Samantha, or the psychopaths Stick hired."

I'd never heard anyone call out Stanley before. At least not anyone I'd ever seen again. I shrank into the seat trying to hide and waited for an explosion even bigger than the one we'd just seen.

Instead Stanley chuckled. Terry even joined him although I'm pretty sure the half-baked moron laughed at almost anything.

"Of course we knew Samantha was boning Butch," he said. Terry giggled louder at "boning". Stanley quieted him with a glare then continued. "We knew Stick's new guys were sniffing around Jimmy's business looking for an easy score. We knew people would be fixated on the safe. Hell, we counted on it. The only thing we didn't know was how much you and your boyfriend would screw things up."

I looked at Dea's face and saw she wasn't satisfied with his answer. I closed my eyes and opened a psychic connection with her.

"Shut up. Shut up! For the love of god, SHUT UP!" I mentally screamed at Dea.

She was not on the same wavelength. Not at all.

"You still have no idea what was really in the safe," she said smugly.

"You don't get it," Stan growled. "The safe was a convenient diversion. We didn't care."

"It's more important than you think," she said quietly.

Stanley began to speak again but was cut short by his phone ringing. He turned away and answered it.

"Yeah."

A muffled voice spoke for a few seconds. I was envious of the gutsy bastard on the other end: he hung up on Stanley.

"Change of plans. Terry, we're done ghosting. Take us to Buffalo Bill's," Stanley said.

I closed my eyes and clenched my jaw at yet another fucking change of plans.

"We're alive, we're alive!" Terry shouted.

"Shut up, Terry," Stanley snapped. Then he made it clear Q & A time was finished by leaning back into the seat and closing his eyes. Snores that could wake the dead rumbled the car just a few seconds later.

Chapter Thirty-seven

Terry lazily returned us to Downtown. He coasted to a stop at the corner entrance of the Interstate Building. The neon beer signs hanging in the windows were off, their tubing a sad, dull, milky white.

Stanley handed Terry a Benjamin while Dea and I got out of the cab.

"Drive around for a while, Terry. I'll call ya."

"Sure, Stan-man. Peace," drifted out the response just before Stanley slammed the door.

An orange flare lit up the interior of the cab for a moment then the dingy taxi drove away.

Stanley ushered us inside the building. Rex washed glasses at the far end of the bar. The TV above him glowed with a rerun of the holiday classic, *Scrooged*.

I paused to order a beer. Stanley stopped me.

"No time for that. Upstairs."

"Upstairs?" I asked, raising my eyebrows.

"Yeah, Jimmy's office. Now."

My stomach flipflopped. I'd only been upstairs a few times and even then, only to the reception area. This was like being called to the principal's office – a principal rumored to exercise capital punishment.

The buffalo head on the wall silently watched us walk through the rest of the bar, weaving around tables with chairs flipped upside down on them. We trudged up the stairs in the far back corner, the aged oak treads accenting our every step with creeks, groans, and pops.

The stairway dumped us into the reception area. A worn Persian rug covered most of the hardwood floor. Lawyers book cases lined the wood-paneled walls protecting hundreds of books behind their glass fronts. The rest of the tiny room was furnished with a small antique walnut pedestal desk backed by a sturdy walnut swivel chair. A pair of simple ladderback chairs faced the desk. Venetian blinds covered two side windows; harsh blue light from the street crept through their slats. The glowing green shade of a vintage brass banker's desk lamp provided the only other illumination.

Behind the desk was the doorway to Jimmy's office. I'd never seen it open.

It was open.

Stanley led us past the empty receptionist's desk into Jimmy's office. It was like stepping into the Roarin' 20s room inside the Museum of Contemporary History. In a way it even reminded me a little of the secret room in the building on Main Street only slightly more "lived in."

Jimmy sat behind a massive desk that appeared to be a twin to the one in The Library. His hair was damp and he'd changed into his usual going-to-the-yacht-club attire of khaki pants and peach colored Oxford shirt. The floor was covered with not one but two giant Persian rugs. Several bronze wall sconces provided light and weird shadows to the room. One sidewall was a continuous bookcase filled with old, leather-bound books; Dea drooled at the sight of them like she was looking at Hot Jesus/Luke the Bounty Hunter. The other sidewall was lined with curio cabinets, each filled with Kansas City memorabilia including campaign pins from the early 1900s, advertising trinkets from long-gone businesses, and in the case nearest Jimmy, a human skull with a small hole in its forehead. The skull strongly resembled one I'd seen in a newspaper article about a skeleton found under the runway pavement at the Downtown Airport. I started to ask about it but quickly decided I really didn't want to know.

A single window was behind Jimmy but it was bricked over. My eyes widened at the sight of two Thompson sub-machine guns and a Colt .45 pistol hanging from small wooden pegs on the wall above Jimmy's head.

Several high-back chairs formed an arc in front of his desk. They looked like electric chairs upholstered with my grandmother's curtains. Stick, wearing the same sweatshirt and jeans he wore at his garage, fidgeted uncomfortably in one of them, intentionally looking away from Jimmy.

Jimmy's munchkin warrior of an attorney, Alex Meezer, sat in another. At just a few millimeters over 5 feet tall and a couple bullet slugs over a hundred pounds, she talks – shouts actually – like she's much larger. Her short, spikey crew cut hints at her previous career as

235

a Marine; the dark brown waxed canvas barn coat she wore covered the Eagle, Globe, and Anchor tattoo I knew to be on her right forearm that confirms she's always faithful to the Corps. The blue chambray shirt, faded jeans, and scuffed hiking boots she wore looked casual enough but she sat rigidly in the chair as though she was about to be electrocuted. She rolled her eyes when she saw me. I replied with a fake smile under a crinkled nose.

"Sit," he ordered politely – politely, but firmly.

Stanley flopped into the chair on Jimmy's right. He reached to his throat and undid his bowtie and popped the top button on his shirt. Dea and I shuffled across the old rug and dropped into chairs between Stick and Alex.

The old chairs were like a hormonal teenaged boy: stiff and uncomfortable. I tried to cross my legs but no matter how I shifted I always banged my knee into the armrest. I gave up and sat flat-footed.

Dea glanced at the empty chair between Alex and Stanley – Nik's chair. Her eyes turned glassy for a few seconds then she clenched her jaw and stared at Jimmy.

Jimmy looked down at his desk then spoke quietly. "My plans the last couple of days haven't, ah, worked out quite as I expected."

"Ya think?" someone whispered loud enough for everyone in the room to hear. It was one of those "oh shit" moments where I realized my mouth said exactly what I was thinking without really thinking. I folded my hands on my lap and looked down.

Jimmy ignored my interruption and continued.

"In the morning," he said glancing at his watch, "or rather later this morning I'm having a press conference to announce our real discovery."

This appeared to be old news to Stanley, Stick, and Alex. I was confused. Dea looked perplexed as well.

"The Bosses' Library contained a treasure of actual books. Hundreds of first editions – some of them possibly the only surviving copies. All of them extremely rare. We will donate them all to the university to either preserve or sell to fund the school's arts programs."

I was shocked. I'd been knocked onto a pile of priceless books and my face shoved into a valuable first edition. And yet my back still hurt.

"What about the safe?" Dea asked. "That's what people expect to hear about. What was in the safe? It certainly wasn't gold or old guns from a massacre."

The light was low so I can't be certain, but when Dea said "guns" I swore both Jimmy and Stanley glanced at the firearms mounted on the wall behind Jimmy. That was probably my imagination though.

"As far as the public knows it was just old tavern records from decades ago," Jimmy said very matter-of-factly. He leaned forward. "The safe was supposed to keep the media away from the building while we cataloged the books and moved them to a controlled space. I didn't expect someone would be dumb enough to believe it held gold."

"That's bullshit!" I heard myself say out loud again. I don't remember standing up but there I was out of my chair.

"Sit down, ay," Stick said dismissively.

The brain trust laughed. But I didn't. I was tired, sore, and apparently not as calloused as the others to the fact Nik's chair was empty. Empty because he was blown to pieces. Along with my ex-girlfriend. Yeah, he was a surly, old, alleged hit-man and she was a batshit crazy gold-digger, but they were still people we knew. People we knew murdered right in front of us.

"I'm glad you find this funny – funny that Nik is gone," I said sharply. My lips twitched with the sensation of a small furry paw covering them – Patch letting me know I was treading on thin eggshells.

"Fuck this. Wait...no, fuck you," I said jabbing a finger in Stick's direction. Then I swept it past the rest of the brain trust. "Fuck you, fuck you, and, oh yeah," I said finishing with Jimmy, "especially fuck you."

Everyone looked at me first with surprise then with expectation. I blundered on anyway but with less gusto.

"If you didn't expect someone to try to steal the damn thing you wouldn't have had a fake and hidden the real one."

I locked eyes with Jimmy. He responded like a teacher to a failing student.

"Word leaked we found a safe," he said patiently. "The public wouldn't understand the real contents so I provided a substitute that was less...provocative."

I felt two paws cover my mouth. They were in vain.

"So, Nik and Samantha died because you, the great Jimmy Penders, is smarter than everyone else," I spat.

Jimmy stared hard into my eyes, his expression strained.

"Yes, they are gone because of me," he said quietly.

Uncomfortable silence filled the room. Dea's eyes were bright and sympathetic to my words. I expected Stanley to rip out my liver for speaking my mind. However, he stared at the ceiling above Jimmy's head. I had a feeling in this instance he felt the same as I did. Stick's eyes shot daggers at me but he stayed slouched in his uncomfortable chair. Ironically, I think Nik probably would have slit my throat for my insolence on his behalf.

Jimmy looked around the room to see if anyone else felt the need to pile on; no one did.

"I talked with Sgt. Stevens. Once the fire was out they found the remains of two bodies in the car. He won't notify Assante until they are identified – probably later today. He was sending an officer to Duluth to find the bounty hunter and his skips."

I found it interesting the shitbags from Duluth were now "the bounty hunter's skips" and not "Stick's employees." I kept that observation to myself.

"Fortunately," Jimmy continued, "Stevens was there with us when it happened but I still expect him to contact all of us with questions."

Alex stood up and reminded everyone she was still Corps to the bone.

"You all will lay low for a few days," she barked.

"Stick," she said curtly, "you and your crew lock up the garage and scatter."

Stick smiled at the instructions. Then Jimmy added "Keep them local, though. You too. I mean it."

Stick bobbed his head sharply then rested his chin on his fist and fumed.

"Stanley," Alex said, "work from home. Keep helping Handz with his new charity."

Stanley, obviously displeased, frowned but nodded slowly.

"Dea," she said surprising Dea because they'd never actually met, "stay with Hook and help him look after his cat."

She started to protest but Jimmy gave her a look that said they weren't kidding.

"Don't worry. My people will take care of your coffee shop."

She accepted defeat and slumped into her chair.

Alex reached into her satchel and pulled out a dark brown pocket folder, its flap held shut with a black string. She frisbeed it into my chest. "Hook, read this and just–" she said, her eyes darting as she searched for the right words, "–just fucking stay put and for god's sake don't touch anything."

A fuzzy paw pressed against my lips again. This time I kept my trap shut.

Chapter Thirty-eight

Terry's cab was idling at the curb when we stepped outside of Bill's. I glanced at Dea; her look of concern matched mine. I considered walking home but heavy snow was falling again and the wind had picked up. Reluctantly, we got into the backseat of the car. It smelled of "incense" and a fresh gold cardboard tree dangled from the rearview mirror.

The old taxi sagged considerably when Stanley dropped his large frame into the front seat. I was relieved to hear him say, "Western Auto Lofts."

"Yessir," Terry mumbled and carefully guided the car down the street.

We drove in silence which, after our "meeting" in Jimmy's office, was just fine with me.

The silence didn't agree with Dea though.

"Stanley," she said.

"Oh fuck me," I thought.

When Dea punched me in the thigh I realized I said that out loud, too. She further surprised me with her next question.

"What's up with the tux?"

Stanley chuckled at the new direction of her curiosity.

"I was at a fundraiser with Handz Middlebrook."

The memory of him being tazed by several KCPD cops during a nasty traffic stop popped into my head.

"That screwup?" I asked.

"Shut your hole," Stanley snapped. "He's a good kid, just needs a little direction. Jimmy and I helped him start the Helping Handz Foundation. It'll keep him busy and out of trouble."

"Maybe you should start a charity," Dea whispered to me.

Stanley overheard her suggestion.

"He *is* a charity case," Stanley said.

Our stoner cabbie coasted to a stop in front of the loft before I could reply.

"Stay home," Stanley ordered sharply. "And stay safe," he added in a more concerned tone.

Dea went to her apartment to fetch extra clothes. I went straight to my loft.

Patch was waiting. He purred loudly when I opened the door – even louder when I gave him several pieces of Kitty Krak and topped off his food and water.

I tossed the file folder onto the coffee table on top of the small mountain of other things I needed to read then dropped onto the couch. Feathers puffed out of the bullet holes. Again.

Patch darted into the living room and jumped onto my chest. He curled up and closed his eye while I petted him. The next thing I knew Dea was beside me. The television was on and Patch had moved to her lap.

"You almost slept through the press conference," she said.

Jimmy and his historian girlfriend from the university were behind a podium at the old building.

I pointed to the TV and said "She and Jimmy are dating."

Dea squinted at her twin on the screen. "Her? She seems a little plain."

I started to reply but had a rare flash of common sense and decided I shouldn't. Dea turned up the volume so we could hear better. We leaned forward and listened.

"...books worth millions were discovered in a sealed room," Jimmy was saying. "Many of them are rare first editions. Some may even be one-of-a-kind. We have moved all of them to the university. We expect most of them to be kept in the special collections. Some may be sold to fund scholarship programs."

A smattering of applause interrupted Jimmy's speech. He paused for it to die out.

"What about the safe?" a reporter shouted out.

"The safe was opened last night but unfortunately it only contained paperwork for a downtown bar. At least it wasn't empty though," he said eliciting some chuckles from the audience.

Dea, visibly disappointed, muted the set.

"That was underwhelming," she said.

"That's my boss," I replied with a shrug. Then I fell asleep again.

I woke up several hours later. Dea had moved to the bedroom

which seemed like a really good idea. I got up to join her. The Jimmy Phone buzzed on the coffee table. I considered ignoring the call but relented after the third ring and answered it.

Stanley was on the other end. "The service for Nik is tomorrow at 10," he said quietly. "We'll be at the Calvary Cemetery at the bottom of the hill. You can leave the apartment to attend."

CLICK.

I felt like I'd been kicked in the stomach. I curled up with Dea and Patch on the bed and fell asleep with them in my arms.

Chapter Thirty-nine

The next morning, I dug out my Wedding-and-Funerals suit from the far end of my closet. Dea wore a black dress and matching jacket. Without Nik to call – and unsure how to contact Terry – we had to Uber to the cemetery.

The grounds of Calvary Cemetery are large but new graves are easy to find in the winter time. I easily spotted the small mound of brown dirt on the snow-covered grass and directed our driver to it.

The Uber driver dropped us off behind a red Lexus that was parked behind two new, black Escalades. Dea and I walked down a small hill to where Jimmy, Stanley, Alex, Stick, and Dorothy stood. In front of them was a maroon and gold casket. A pair of Stick's men were also there but stood several feet away from the grave. I didn't know if that was out of respect or if they were standing guard.

Dea and I joined the group. A few snowflakes floated through the gray sky.

Jimmy looked at each of us then spoke.

"Nik was a man of few words. I will honor him in the same manner. He was a good, loyal man. We will miss him."

"Amen," said Stanley.

Stick still looked pissed. He wordlessly bowed his head for a moment. A tear ran down Dorothy's cheek. I looked at my shoes and bit my lip. Dea squeezed my hand.

The solemnness of the moment was broken by the chirp of tires on pavement. A black Chevy Suburban with ebony tinted windows skidded to a stop on the hill above the grave site. We all looked at one another trying to see if we'd forgotten someone.

Two very average looking men in black suits and even blacker sunglasses walked down the hill to the gravesite. They looked over our little group, nodded slightly to each other, and then stepped over to Dorothy.

"Ma'am, we're very sorry for your loss," the average height one said.

"John, er, Nik, I mean, was a great man," the averager height one said.

The first glared at him through his sunglasses then handed Dorothy a large manila envelope.

"The President sends his regards."

They nodded to Dorothy, turned curtly, and walked away. We watched with slack jaws as they climbed back into the Suburban. The rear tires chirped again as they sped away.

Dorothy looked at the envelope. It was battered and dingy. The corners were worn away. It wasn't even sealed - the short, red string dangled uselessly from a cardboard button on the flap. The second button below it was missing.

She pushed the flap up and withdrew a single sheet of light

beige parchment. Dorothy's hands shook so it was difficult to read. Across the top in large print was "Executive Grant of Clemency." I saw the words "...for service to this country..." above "Ivan Kuznetsova, a.k.a. Nikola Andropov." At the bottom was a large, gold foil presidential seal next to the honest-to-god Commander in Chief's signature.

Dorothy, overwhelmed with emotion, bear hugged Jimmy. She hugged Stanley and gently shook Stick's hand. Then she walked up the hill to her car.

I was dumbfounded. I looked to Stanley and asked the obvious question: "Who the hell is Ivan Kuznetsova?"

Stanley rolled his eyes. Instead of calling me an idiot or dumbass or whatever insult he had queued up, he shook his head and walked away several steps. Stick and Alex followed him. They chatted quietly while I wrapped my brain around "Ivan Kuznetsova."

Dea approached Jimmy and reached into her purse. Alarm klaxons screeched in my noggin. I reached for her but she brushed me away.

"Jimmy," she said, thrusting the scorched papers toward him. "What do these mean?"

"Nothing. They mean nothing now."

"Jimmy, they're ballots. I saw hundreds of them. All of them from 1948. All of them marked Dewey/Warren."

"Thousands actually," Jimmy corrected. "33,000 votes scattered around California, Illinois, and Ohio. Just enough to flip the electoral college to a different result."

Dea silently pondered Jimmy's new information. I pondered how the hell he knew how many there were.

"They stole ballots?! They stole the election?!"

"Perhaps," Jimmy said with a slight frown. "Or they might have been fakes, ready to be stuffed into ballot boxes to ensure Dewey actually did beat Truman. I imagine that threat would have carried a lot of weight."

The iconic image of the incorrect newspaper headline flashed into my head: a failed haberdasher from Missouri holding up a newspaper, its headline falsely announcing his defeated foe was the winner. I wondered if maybe that reporter was the only one who really had it right. Dea considered Jimmy's theory but still looked skeptical.

"Or, as you suggest," Jimmy said, "they might have been real ballots – ballots stolen to ensure Missouri's favorite son became president. Who's to say which it was? It didn't work anyway – Harry Truman never did anything to save the Bosses from being deposed. And really, what good would it do to stir this up now?"

Dea looked shocked. I'm not sure why – Kansas City used to be second only to the dead voting army in Chicago when it came to rigging elections. I'm sure she had more questions but Jimmy wasn't in the mood for more answers. He crumpled the ancient ballots and tossed them into the hole beneath Nik's casket.

The three of us stared at the grave. I wondered if maybe John/Ivan/Nik's coffin should've been red, white, and blue instead.

The silence of our reverie was shattered by three Kansas City Police cruisers, red and blue lights rolling, roaring up to the grave site.

The front doors of the lead squad car burst open. Lieutenant Assante jogged around from the passenger side then ran directly at us like a crazed child chasing a twenty-dollar bill in a hurricane. Holstein, gripping his belt to keep his pants from dropping, lumbered along behind him.

Jimmy and the others shook their heads at the intrusion – but none of them looked particularly surprised.

Assante went straight for Jimmy. He was red with fury. I figured Stevens finally told him what happened to Samantha – my heart thumped as he drew near. He had one hand on his gun, the other on his night stick; as furious as he looked I wasn't sure if what little professionalism he had would keep him from using one or the other – or both.

When he got to Jimmy he just stopped in front of him. He stood up straight and looked up at Jimmy's chin. Then, in a move that caught everyone off guard, he pulled his night stick and clubbed Jimmy in the kidney. When Jimmy doubled over he brought the stick down on Jimmy's shoulder blades, dropping him to his knees.

"Jimmy Penders, you are under arrest," he said while Holstein fumbled hand cuffs around Jimmy's wrists.

"For WHAT?!" Alex roared.

"Go to hell, Meezer," Assante snapped.

"Sonny," she yelled back, using the grade school nickname she knew he detested, "You uncuff my client or–"

"Your client stole a car, kidnapped my daughter, and had her murdered. I ought to put a bullet in him right now."

His eyes blazed. I thought he might actually do it. He and Sam never seemed to get along but I guess he cared for her more than he let on. I almost pitied him.

"I've finally got you, Penders. The van stolen from the impound lot was on your property," he sneered.

So, Samantha's death was just part of a convenient excuse for Assante to finally arrest Jimmy. My pity for the heartless old fuck vanished.

Two more officers I didn't know walked up.

"Them, too," Assante said, nodding at Stanley and Stick.

Dorothy, Dea, and I watched in disbelief as the officers cuffed them but without using their batons first. Stan and Stick looked plenty pissed but didn't flinch.

"Nothing!" Alex barked. "You say nothing unless I'm there!"

The officers led Stick and Stanley back to their car.

Assante pointed at me, so angry he could barely speak. "You. You're worthless – jail's too good for you. I'll take care of you later." He shoved Jimmy back toward Holstein's cruiser. Holstein snorted at us then followed Assante to the car.

The police cars sped away with my boss and his most trusted men. I was stunned beyond words. Not even the sarcastic words that usually burst into my head.

"Well," Alex said snapping me out of my fugue. "Now what?"

The mouthpiece asked me for suggestions – that was rich.

"Huh?" was all I could think to say.

"Now. What?" She repeated. "Didn't you open the folder?"

she asked suspiciously.

An image of the unopened folder laying on top of Dea's unread books floated through my skull.

"Um, sure," I fibbed. I wondered why the hell people give me things to read when I obviously never do.

"You moron," she said, her eyelids fluttering with exasperation. "Your contract is in it. Jimmy put you in charge of all his businesses if he and Stanley aren't able to run things."

My knees buckled. Dea caught me before I fell into Nik's grave.

"Aw, shit," she said.


The End

## Epilogue

I strutted into Buffalo Bills like I owned the place. Technically speaking, I kinda did but the staff and regulars ignored me like I was still just another schmuck off the street.

The first Monday after New Year's is always slammed and this one wasn't any different. It was lunch rush and the place was packed with lawyers, cops, and low-level federal functionaries. I spotted one open stool near the far end of the bar – a rarity for such a busy day. I headed toward it, hoping no one else would snag it first. My pace picked up when I spotted the stunning redhead in the seat next to it.

I dropped my keister into the empty seat. The redhead was a petite hourglass wrapped in form-hugging jeans and an emerald sweater. The 3-inch heels on her boots didn't seem very practical for the weather but they sure looked great on her. Her eyes were the same color as her sweater and sparkled. Unfortunately, I noticed them last when she busted me finishing my down-up appraisal of her form.

I turned crimson.

"Uh, hi. I'm Hook," I squeaked.

"Stacy," she replied curtly then took a sip from the glass of water in front of her.

She had the air of a lady who's not easy to impress. I tried anyway.

"This, uh, is my bar," I said, stretching the truth just a little.

Rex overheard me. "No it isn't," he snorted.

"Hey, don't make me fire you," I said with a nervous chuckle. I looked at the stunning Stacy and added "we kid a lot." Rex walked to the other end of the bar while I wondered if I really could fire the crochety old fart.

Stacy smirked slightly then looked away.

I focused my attention to a menu, quietly hoping none of the staff would tell Dea that I spoke to a gorgeous redhead. I glared at Rex as he pointedly ignored my signal that I wanted to order.

My left ear tingled. I snapped my head to the left in response to the sensation of a small feline paw tapping at it. Of course, there was no cat there. Instead I saw a painfully familiar woman walk through the door. My heart stopped.

Her hair was platinum blonde and partially covered by a dark silk scarf. She wore large, dark sunglasses that obscured half her face. Black slacks and a dark blue blouse peeked out from under her unbuttoned wool trench coat. From across the room I could smell her perfume: the scent of 1000 flowers. I'd smelled that fragrance dozens of times; it was to me like fresh catnip is to Patch.

She quickly scanned the room, eventually spotting me at the bar. She walked straight to me, stopping right beside my barstool. Even though her disguise was pretty lame, inexplicably, no one else in the bar but me noticed her.

"Samantha?" I stammered, "I watched...you're...how, uh, but...you're dead?"

As she always did when we were a couple, she ignored my jabbering.

"Hook...Hook, I'm in trouble," she said pleadingly.

My mouth moved but nothing came out. Like so often happens when a dead ex-girlfriend comes into your bar and tells you she needs help, I didn't know what to say. Suddenly the disinterested redhead beside me took interest.

"You," she said pointing at Samantha, "you don't belong here."

Samantha winced and took a step backward. I looked around the room, hoping the commotion unfolding by my barstool didn't draw too much attention. Everyone continued with their lunch as if nothing unusual was happening. Even Rex continued ignoring me the way he always did.

Stacy raised her right hand and pointed a polished, iridescent gray stone at Sam. Sam staggered back as though she'd been punched in the throat.

The redhead's beautiful green eyes flashed like Heineken somehow bottled lightning.

"It's time for you to move along. Don't come back here. And stay away from Hook," she commanded.

I stared at the rock in her hand. A pale blue-green glow shimmered around the stone for a moment then dissipated.

My jaw dropped again. I looked at Stacy, "What the..." I

started but didn't finish when I realized Samantha was gone. I looked furtively around the room; she was nowhere to be seen. It was as though she had never even been in the bar.

I returned my attention to the redheaded stranger. She placed a twenty-dollar bill on the bar under the water glass and pushed herself away from the bar.

"That won't last forever. Here," she said placing the polished stone in front of me. "It's labradorite. Keep it with you always – it'll help keep that skeeze-weasel out of your head."

I was as confused as an old hillbilly at a soccer match but before I could ask any questions, she turned for the door. She paused after a couple of steps and looked back at me.

"Oh, and tell Patch that Thor says they're even."

I stared with confusion as she strode out of the bar without looking back. I picked up the stone and rubbed it with my thumb for a few seconds. I felt pressure on my chest and suddenly had trouble breathing. While I tried to make sense of what happened a paw thumped me on the nose.

I lurched in confusion. I looked around; gradually it all made sense. Samantha was gone. Stacy the strange redhead was gone. The whole damn bar was gone. I was in my bed and Patch was sitting on my chest.

I sighed. My furry sidekick rescued me from a nightmare once again. I scratched him under his chin until he purred.

"Thanks, buddy," I said.

"Meow," he replied then padded over to the nightstand.

He started batting at something. I rolled my eyes then leaned across the bed to move my keys away from his mischievous paws. Except he wasn't playing with my keys. He wasn't even warning me of an incoming phone call.

He was playing with a polished, iridescent gray stone. He paused and looked at me.

The dream was still fresh in my memory. I squinted quizzically at my little side-kick.

"Patch, who the hell is Thor?" I asked.

He tilted his head and winked. Or blinked – hell, I still can't tell the difference.

"Meow."

\* \* \*

Thanks for reading.  Stay tuned for more Hook and Patch.

Jeff

41593692R00156

Made in the USA
Middletown, DE
08 April 2019